The New Life of Hugo Gardner

The New Life
of Hugo Gardner

A NOVEL

LOUIS BEGLEY

NAN A. TALESE | DOUBLEDAY

NEW YORK

www.nanatalese.com

DOUBLEDAY is a registered trademark of Penguin Random House LLC. Nan A. Talese and the colophon are trademarks of Penguin Random House LLC.

Jacket photographs: man on bench © Magnito/Shutterstock; dog © Eric Isselee/Shutterstock; Eiffel Tower © r.classen/ Shutterstock; background © Cafe Racer/Shutterstock
Jacket design by Michael J. Windsor

LIBRARY OF CONGRESS CATALOGING-IN-PUBLICATION DATA
Names: Begley, Louis, author.
Title: The new life of Hugo Gardner : a novel / Louis Begley.
Description: First edition. | New York : Nan A. Talese/ Doubleday, [2020]
Identifiers: LCCN 2019019594| ISBN 9780385545624 (hardcover) | ISBN 9780385545679 (eBook)
Subjects: | GSAFD: Satire.
Classification: LCC PS3552.E373 N49 2020 | DDC 813/.54—dc23
LC record available at https://lccn.loc.gov/2019019594

MANUFACTURED IN THE UNITED STATES OF AMERICA

1 3 5 7 9 10 8 6 4 2

First Edition

For Anka always,

and, once again, for Grisha

We have lingered in the chambers of the sea
By sea-girls wreathed with seaweed red and brown
Till human voices wake us, and we drown.

—T. S. ELIOT, "THE LOVE SONG OF J. ALFRED PRUFROCK"

The New Life of Hugo Gardner

I

THE TELEPHONE RANG just as I was about to go out to lunch. In the caller-ID window, NY followed by a number I didn't recognize. I shrugged. To hell with it. I'll answer.

Is Hugo Gardner available?

A voice hard to classify. Tough, no effort to make himself pleasant. Perhaps a fund-raiser for retired police chiefs.

Who's calling?

Attorney William Sweeney. Is Hugo Gardner available?

I admitted I was and asked what I could do for him.

I represent your wife, Mrs. Valerie Gardner. Does an attorney represent you?

I'm not sure I understand, I told him. Why are you asking whether I have a lawyer? What are you representing my wife about?

You'll understand that I can't discuss a case with a party who is already represented by an attorney. Anyway, it would be better if I spoke to your attorney.

Well, I replied, you had better tell me what this is all about. Depending on what you say, I may or may not think I need a lawyer. So please go ahead.

All right, Hugo. It's my understanding that your wife is away for a few days on business. Is that right?

I was about to ask this fellow to address me as Mr. Gardner. Instead, I said, Yes, that's right.

Mrs. Gardner wishes to obtain a divorce. She has asked me to inform you and to urge you to retain counsel so we can get the work done promptly and smoothly. That's the reason for my call. Mrs. Gardner told me that your email address is hugo.gardner1932@gmail.com. If that's correct, I'll send you an email with my contact information as soon as we hang up, so that your attorney can reach out to me.

Wait a moment, please, I said. What do you mean: my wife wants to divorce me? I've never heard any such thing.

She thought you might act surprised. She wants a divorce on the grounds of your cruel and inhuman treatment of her, and the irretrievable breakdown in your relationship. You surely recognize that this is so.

Like hell I do.

Let's not argue, Hugo. You'll get my email. After that I'll expect to hear from your attorney.

He hung up.

I was going to have lunch alone at my club and afterward see a photography show at MoMA. All that could wait. Twelve-fifteen. Therefore nine-fifteen in San Francisco. I called Valerie's cell-phone number. She wasn't an early riser.

I guessed she'd be having breakfast in bed in her room at the Fairmont. Several rings. Was she in the bathroom, or had she decided not to answer, once she saw that the call was from me? But no, she answered. A weary: Yes.

Hello, Valerie, I said, I've just had the strangest conversation with a man called Sweeney. He claims he's your lawyer and you want a divorce. What's going on?

What's going on is that it's just as Bill Sweeney told you. I can't go on living with you. I'd rather be dead. I want a divorce, *le plus vite possible.*

Why she should find it useful to insert French into the conversation was beyond me. The whole thing was beyond me.

I must be dreaming, I replied. You left two days ago. On the morning plane. Very affectionate goodbye. We made love the night before. You certainly seemed to enjoy it. I told you I was getting tickets for *Eugene Onegin* and you said that was a great idea. Tickets for you and me. What happened between then and now? Is this some sort of bad joke?

What happened is that I let you fuck me last Tuesday the way I usually do to get some peace and some rest before going on a trip that's important to me professionally. Do you understand what that means? Do you ever pay attention? Do you ever notice what goes on around you? Don't you know that living with you is like living with a corpse? Not even a zombie. An unburied corpse! I can't stand you, I haven't been able to stand you for years! You don't know that, imbecile?

No, I don't know any such thing. Why didn't you speak to me about it before sending Mr. Sweeney?

Are you joking? And have you lecture me for three hours about how I'm wrong? This was the only way to do it.

Really, I said. Do the kids know how you feel? Do they know about the divorce idea?

Barbara sure knows how I feel. Do you think she's feeble-minded? I haven't told her yet that I'm definitely leaving you, but Roddy's probably clued her in. He recommended Bill Sweeney.

I see, I said, pulled out a stool from under the kitchen counter, and sat down.

I see, I repeated. And what will be your next steps?

It was a stupid question, I realized, but I'd spoken as though on some sort of autopilot.

I'm returning to the city next Wednesday. I want to come by the apartment on Thursday around eleven to take some of my clothes and other things. It would be better if you weren't there. Mrs. Perez can make sure I don't steal the Gardner family silver. You'd better put your lawyer in touch with Bill Sweeney. I suppose you'll use that idiot Weinstein.

Larry Weinstein became the lawyer who took care of my will and the trusts I'd set up for the kids after the law firm that my father and later I had used decided to shut down its trusts and estate department. Larry had been recommended by my tax accountant, and he turned out to be just fine, in fact a good deal brighter than his predecessor, a giggly squash-playing Yalie. Mrs. Perez was our housekeeper.

As it happened, she'd informed me some hours earlier that she had her period and wouldn't be coming to work. This was Thursday. Mrs. Perez's periods had a way of going on and on, but really, till next Thursday... If she was still out on some new pretext, I'd wait for Valerie at the apartment. Perhaps I'd be there in any case. That depended on what Larry said.

I managed to croak goodbye and hung up. There was nothing else to say.

No kidding was what Larry said after he'd heard my story.

I'd gone to see him that very afternoon, directly from my favorite neighborhood hamburger joint where I had a thousand-plus-calorie Cobb salad, a draft beer, and a double espresso. To hell with the calories. Even if I put on a pound or two or three, I'd still be plenty thin. Anyway, who was there to care about my waistline? It had been my plan to lunch at the club, but the thought of sitting down at the members' table and being obliged to talk to my neighbors repelled me. I drank my coffee, paid the bill, and made my way to Larry's office.

I didn't reply, so he said it again: No kidding. And you had no inkling of any of this?

I shook my head.

Does she have someone else?

I have no idea, I replied. It's a bolt out of the blue. If she has someone, she hasn't let on. I should add that I'm not suspicious. I'd probably be the last to know. Let me ask you something. You know my son, Rod. I remember having you go over my will and my trust with him.

Larry nodded.

Do you find what he has done natural? Believable? Getting a divorce lawyer for his mother without telling me? Without insisting that she let him tell me?

It's strange, Larry replied. I'm not surprised it upsets you. In his defense, he probably thought he was doing you both a favor by steering his mother to Bill Sweeney. Bill comes across as rough, but he is competent and on the whole reasonable. She might have picked someone much, much worse.

I see. So, what happens now?

She's a very forceful person. It sounds to me as though her mind is made up, so there's no point in trying conciliation or mediation. Sweeney will ask you to agree to a separation. Once you sign the agreement, it will be possible, if you don't object—and why would you?—to file for an uncontested divorce. The decree will come through pretty quick.

Without my having given her any cause?

Larry laughed. New York is a no-fault-divorce state. You told me what Sweeney said: inhuman treatment—he means you're mistreating her—and breakdown in your relationship. Under New York law, that's good enough, or bad enough. As you like. I told you that they'll want to go to a separation agreement. That's when you'll hear about how much money she wants, furniture, art, and so forth. The rest of that stuff, who's at fault, are you really a monster, and so forth, will all become irrelevant.

Money?

She'll surely ask for money. Perhaps alimony, perhaps a sum of money, perhaps both.

Even though it's her idea, and I haven't done anything like—I don't know what—adultery? Or even beaten her, hell, hit her, or yelled at her? I'm not a yeller.

He nodded.

And I have to agree to this?

No, but if your wife is determined, and Sweeney doesn't discourage her, you'll end up agreeing to some significant percentage of what she wants or getting into a catfight that may have to be resolved in court.

I don't think I'd want that. Would she?

Hard to tell. You say you had no warning. That may well mean she has somebody, and that somebody is calling the shots. Whatever she asks for will be negotiable to some extent, but I doubt she and Sweeney will accept a flat no.

I thought it over and told him he was probably right.

Are you able to represent me in a case against her? I asked. And is this the sort of work you do?

The answer to both questions is yes, he answered. She's never been my client, so I have no conflict. She's just a beneficiary under your will, which, by the way, you'll want to change pretty quick. And I've done enough separation agreements and divorces to think I can stand up to Sweeney. However, if we see that this will have to be litigated we may want to bring in someone else.

That's the first good news I've had today. I have one more question. Should I be at the apartment when Valerie comes to get her stuff? That's Thursday next week. Should I stay away? What's best?

Let me call Sweeney and tell him I'm on board and that you plan to be present during your wife's visit. Let's see what he says. He may tell me no way, in which case we should avoid a confrontation. Or he may say that in such case he'll accompany her. If that happens, you might decide to have me there as well. By the way, I'll have to ask you to sign an engagement letter.

Right, I said, I'll expect your call and your letter. And now I had better run.

In fact, I had all the time in the world. I wasn't expected anywhere, but I thought I had better leave lest I break down and cry right there, in my lawyer's office.

She did bring Sweeney to the apartment. Not to be outgunned, I had Larry on hand. Thus, both lawyers were treated to the stream of her wisecracks and recriminations. Sweeney had with him a couple of pads of yellow Post-its that Valerie stuck on the stuff she wanted. As she and Sweeney were leaving, Larry said we were taking note of her requests and would respond in due course. This set off an

explosion of sarcasm from Valerie and a speech by Sweeney I didn't listen to. She came back to the apartment twice
more, with Sweeney, and once alone to the house in Bridgehampton. We signed the separation agreement in less than
four weeks' time. I found I had little desire to resist—what
was the point? She took a chunk of my money, although she
was leaving for a man eight or ten years younger than she,
a fellow called Louis Leblanc, the owner of a chic restaurant in Chelsea, with whom she'd already moved in. It had
soon become apparent that she'd been sleeping with him for
some time. She took all the jewelry as well as objets d'art I
had given her during the nearly forty years of our marriage,
and most of the paintings and drawings on the walls of our
apartment and house in Bridgehampton other than my
family portraits (she said that looking at those fucking Bos-
tonians had always made her sick). Thank God, she didn't
have the gall to ask for our apartment (that I bought with
my savings when we moved to the city from my last overseas
posting), or the house in Long Island that I inherited from
my widowed and childless aunt Hester, who was also my
godmother.

It turned out that I am just stupid or old-fashioned enough
to accept subconsciously the proposition that, regardless of
fault or circumstances—Valerie has by now not-insignificant
savings of her own as well as the career she's so concerned
about—the husband should submit to being taken to the
cleaners. Besides, I was in a state of shock compounded
of disbelief and profound sadness. Why was she doing it?

Because I'm a fucking corpse? Granted she is a very shapely and still very pretty sixty-one, and I'm eighty-four; it's also true that I weigh only ten pounds more than when I was on the college squash team, that I'm fit and in good health if you put aside the small matter of cancer cells disporting themselves in my prostate, and that I have a full head of hair. Obviously, those cells are up to no good, but the very civilized urologist who took charge of my nether parts after I got rid of his predecessor, a garrulous and hyper expensive leprechaun, agrees that we should leave bad enough alone. Only he uses an expression more medically and politically correct: he is willing to sanction watchful waiting. Waiting for what? To have me die of other causes? Or to see those little buggers hit the road, penetrate my bones, my liver, or Lord knows what else? That's when I'll treat myself to a first-class ticket to Zurich. One of my old journalist pals will direct me to a discreet clinic to which I will have myself driven after an excellent lunch with my pal at the Drei Könige. It will be a relief to pay my obol to the kindly practitioner and cross the river Styx.

I have mentioned journalist friends. Perhaps I should explain. Right out of college, like practically everyone I knew, I volunteered for the draft, served in the army for two years. After basic training at Fort Dix in New Jersey, I was stationed with Supreme Headquarters Allied Powers Europe in Fontainebleau. There was another draftee at SHAPE who had been two classes ahead of me at Harvard College. We became friends. I still had a few months to serve when he was being demobilized, and, before he left, he said that if I liked he'd try to help me get a job at *Life,* where he'd been working and to which he was returning. I'd been on the college newspaper and jumped at the suggestion. He was as good as his word. A month after the army shipped me back home to New York City I reported for work at the magazine. My parents weren't thrilled—my father, a partner at Morgan Stanley, had expected me to go into finance or the law, and my mother invariably followed his lead—but this was the sort of work I had hoped for. Three years later, just as the glamorous new Time-Life Building opened, I jumped ship—at least, that was how some of my *Life* colleagues put it. In my opinion, joining *Time* was an unhoped-for brilliant promotion. My fluent French, learned at school and polished to a high sheen during the Fontainebleau years, plus, I'm not too modest to say, some native talent, turned me into a foreign correspondent. During a lifelong career at *Time,* having zigzagged over Europe and Latin America, I was successively bureau chief in Paris and Moscow. I had been in Moscow for three years when I was invited to return to New York as a senior editor. A year later, I became the managing editor. In 2005, I retired. This time, I was leaving a sinking ship. Alas, the magazine as I had known it had no future. But I had taken the advice of my investment manager and sold pretty much at the peak all but an insignificant number of the company shares I had accumulated through stock options. The proceeds, added to what I inherited from my parents and my aunt Hester, made me better off than I had expected to be.

Back in the seventies, Valerie had been living in London working for the *LA Times*, lost that job, moved to Paris, and was desperately looking for work when we were introduced by a mutual friend who asked me to help her. I did. Through colleagues, I got her a part-time job on the *Herald Tribune* covering the less highbrow cultural events. One thing led to another. In order to clear the decks, I dumped a French-woman with whom I'd had a long, sexually very satisfying, and easy relationship. Why did I do it? That's a long and confusing story. Valerie was a few years younger than my girlfriend, cute as a button, and so very American! I wanted to have an American girl, an American wife. Our two children, Roddy and Barbara, were both born in Paris. Soon after Barbara's birth, Valerie turned her efforts toward French cuisine, attended Cordon Bleu classes, and, inspired by Julia Child, reinvented herself as a gourmet cook and food writer. A very successful food writer indeed: her last two cookbooks quickly became bestsellers, she landed a *Cook with Valerie* show on NPR, and her backlist, *Authentic Périgord Dishes* and *An American Cooks Koulibiak and Borscht in Moscow*, were reissued and have been selling like meat pierogies. Paradoxically, and in my opinion ungratefully, she based her moral claim to a part of my capital on the proposition that my high standing as a journalist and editor had initially interfered with her work's being appreciated at its full value because reviewers regarded her as my protégée, a mere appendage. Perhaps at the very start? But I would have thought that on the whole my influence, such as it was, gave her the openings she needed and had a distinctively positive effect on her career. I never failed to encourage her. The opportunities to become a gourmet conversant with many cuisines, a chef, and so forth and to meet the food-critic mafia came through me. Was that unfair? An example of male domination of the media at that time? Perhaps, but it wasn't a system I had made, and she certainly was glad to profit from it.

When Larry told me that the divorce had come through without a hitch, I thanked him, called my wine merchant and sent him a bottle of vintage Laurent-Perrier with a nice note I dictated, and then sat down at my desk and put my head in my hands. What was I to do? Celebrate or bewail the departure of a woman I still loved and desired physically after forty years of marriage, the mother of my children? Alone or in the company of friends? Which friend or friends, that was the question. The logical choice, Tim Harris, a college classmate who lived in the city, was still in sufficiently good physical shape to go out and eat and drink, and hadn't begun to lose his mind, had long ago turned into a "let's have lunch together" friend. His wife, whom I've known ever since they got married and have always liked, had made it clear in various ways that it was Valerie who was her friend. They lunched and went to openings and concerts together; when Jill telephoned, and I answered, she barely said hello before asking for Valerie; if we did something as two couples in the evening—an increasingly infrequent occurrence—Jill's conversation and attention centered on Valerie and her culinary exploits. I hadn't minded. Ever since we got married, I had made a conscientious effort to integrate her into the circle of my friends and colleagues. I don't brag about this. It was the right, really necessary, thing to do. She was so much younger and was new to the milieu of mostly older people who, from a professional point of view, had all arrived and, in many cases, had attained some renown. I continued this effort when we came to live in New York City. By that time, she was becoming known as a food writer, but she had never lived in the city and had no friends of her own, whereas I, to be perfectly blunt about it, occu- pied a position of power and eminence, in addition to being New York born and bred. Often a woman new to the city, like Valerie, reconnects with college classmates. But she had gone to Reed College in Oregon, and I don't believe she ever tried to find anyone she'd known there in New York. All this changed radically, of course, with her TV show. She acquired a minor-celebrity status. It became natural that our social life should be defined by Valerie. We entertained a great deal at home; Valerie's cooking was superb and irresistible; we had expert help serving dinner or lunch and cleaning up; and she charmed our new guests as she had from the beginning charmed my old New York friends. As she had enchanted me, when I undertook to help her in Paris. So, when it came right down to it, I didn't have the nerve or perhaps even the desire to call one of my former *Time* colleagues and friends, contemporaries or younger writers and editors who'd worked for me and considered me a mentor, and say, Look, I've got news, Valerie's and my divorce has come through, could we have dinner?

It was too bad. I felt like going to one of my neighborhood bistros (of which there is no lack on Carnegie Hill), or to the Northern Italian restaurant in the Fifties I especially like, and having a martini, a bottle of good wine, and some good talk. But did these guys know about Valerie and me, and hadn't called or emailed to say, for instance, that they were sorry, was there anything they could do, because they'd decided not to get involved? Could it be that they didn't know? I hadn't told anyone except Tim that she had walked out, but that didn't mean she hadn't been talking. Perhaps she had arranged to dine and celebrate, she and her Monsieur Leblanc, with the very couples I had in mind as possible dinner companions. Whatever the reason, I didn't call anyone, and no one called me.

I worked until eight or so on my book—provisional title *The Great Con: How George W. Bush Led Us into War*—and, right here at home, to the accompaniment of my old CD of *Rigoletto*, had not one but two martinis, followed by cold roast chicken and most of a bottle of Burgundy. Long live recorded music! I could listen to one of my favorite operas without facing the horrors of Peter Gelb's new productions at the Met. The book was going well, the research finished except for gaps I could fill as I went along at the New York Public Library or, very often, online. I oscillated between rage at what the Bush-Cheney duo had done to the country and indeed the entire Middle East, and wild merriment at their stupidity. In W's case, the thickheadedness was manifest, displayed in verbal gaffes and pronouncements that were in no time at all mocked by the flow of events. Cheney's fundamental stupidity was more difficult to discern. But it lurked behind the persona of Machiavellian shrewdness he had created and managed to impress on the media and politicians of both parties. How else would one explain the disastrously wrong moves on which he sold W, whether attacking Iraq, or working on "the dark side" and staining the country's honor? I hoped the book would turn out to be good enough to lift me from the dumps into which Valerie's departure and, before that, some of the response to my earlier book had plunged me. That was a study, really a very long essay, centered on Bill Clinton's presidency. I had interviewed him a number of times and had found myself impervious to his charm. In my opinion, he had only one solid accomplishment to his credit: the much-needed tax increase he deftly managed to engineer. His inaction in the case of the genocide in Rwanda and the lateness of his response to the Balkan war were shocking, and his disgraceful personal behavior cheapened the presidency and paved W's way to the White House. It hardly mattered whether these views were right or wrong. When my book was issued, the Clinton machine was already promoting Hillary as the inevitable Democratic candidate in 2016, and it upset her fans among reviewers and political analysts. Not that all reviewers or pundits were part of her claque. I was praised fulsomely in conservative and right-wing quarters—not exactly where I look for approval.

No, there was nothing to celebrate, just a sort of ache in some part of my psyche to assuage. I went to bed slightly tipsy and later than usual. Two generous after-dinner shots of small-batch bourbon did it. I felt sure I'd have no trouble falling asleep and perhaps staying asleep until seven or eight in the morning.

Relax, Hugo, I said to myself. Tomorrow will be another day.

If there was another idiotic cliché that fit the occasion I couldn't think of it.

II

YES, TOMORROW CAME, and it turned out to be a pretty ordinary day in the new life of Hugo Gardner. I was about to squeeze the usual two oranges for my breakfast juice, when the telephone rang. It was Mark Horowitz, recently retired from the *NYT* editorial board, where his beat had been national affairs. His wife, Edie, still taught mathematics at Columbia. I thought they were a fine couple. Mark was inviting me to a party the following Monday.

It will be a mixed group, he announced. The old crowd and some of Edie's colleagues. Lots to eat and lots to drink. No special occasion. Just a party. By the way, someone has told me there's some sort of problem between you and Valerie. We want you to know...

He was clearly going to try to reassure me about wanting me at his party even if I came alone, and I interrupted him, laughing in spite of myself. Yes, I said, that's one way to put it. We're divorced—in fact, the divorce came through yesterday. She left me for a fellow called Louis Leblanc, who owns La Bonne Bouffe down in Chelsea. I believe she's living with him.

I could sense Mark's relief.

That's more or less what I was given to understand, he told me. Anyway, Edie and I are very sorry and hope that you will join us. From eight-thirty to the bitter end. Alone if you like, or with a friend.

I'll be there, I replied. For the moment, there is no friend. It will be just me. Really, I'm delighted to come. Thank you! And do give my love to Edie!

So, the cat was out of the bag. Since Mark knew, even though neither he nor Edie was particularly close to Valerie, people were talking about us, probably people I wouldn't have thought could be interested in us as a subject of gossip. The good news was that I didn't need to tell acquaintances I ran into that she and I had split. I could quietly assume that they already knew. The bad news was what they might be saying about us.

I was mulling this over as I drank my orange juice, when the phone rang again. I looked at the caller-ID window. P. LUDINGTON. I said, Hello, Penny!

She sounded out of breath; always had, even in the old days at Radcliffe; it didn't necessarily mean she had been running. It was her way of sounding sexy. Ever since I've known her, she had succeeded. Hugo, she whispered. Will you be out at the beach this weekend? I've heard about Valerie. How perfectly awful! You must be very upset.

What's the weather forecast? I asked in return.

Perfect, she assured me. Sunny and on the warm side.

If the forecast holds, I said, I'll be out. I've hardly been to the house this winter. I suppose it's still there. Someone— one of my house watchers—probably would have let me know if it had burned down or the pipes had burst!

Then you'll come to dinner on Saturday? Just a few people. Eight o'clock?

I'd like that.

Hugo, why did Valerie do it?

Pursuit of happiness. An American right.

She had a good deal with you, Hugo, and she knew it. Everyone knew it. A really stupid move, if you ask me. Be sure to write the date in your calendar. Saturday, at eight. Very casual.

Duly noted.

I had gone to Bridgehampton for the long summer season soon after the negotiation with Valerie and her lawyer ended and I signed the separation agreement, and, once there, had done what I've always done, except for modifications due to the fact that, for the first time since I inherited the house a year or so after I married Valerie, I was there alone. Without Valerie or children or grandchildren. Without Valerie fretting about her dinner parties or the recipe for her newest dish. That was all right. First thing in the morning, I'd go to the bottom of the driveway, pick up the *Times*, and make my breakfast. Then, on the days when Gloria, our Bridge-hampton housekeeper, wasn't supposed to come, or she had texted that she'd be late because of traffic or car trouble, I'd pick up in the kitchen and make my bed. Then I shaved, usually took a shower, and went to the beach. The Bridgehampton beach is less than a stately ten-minute bicycle ride away, but I'd go to Gibson Lane, which is farther, and I'd drive. I've never much liked bicycling, and I particularly don't like "sharing the road" with the kind of drivers who now infest the Hamptons, pushy goons in showy cars. The ocean was as warm as it gets around here. I'd leave the tote bag with my towel, swimming trunks to change into after my swim, and a comb a few hundred feet from the beach entrance and walk east, well past Peters Pond toward the modern brick house above the dune that had been the most handsome structure there until new owners defaced it with incomprehensibly ugly remodeling. If the sand was hard, I'd push on to Georgica. Back at the point of beginning, I'd stash my shirt in the tote and run into the surf—unless it was too wild. The days when I'll still be able to do this are counted, so I make the most of my time in the waves. Usually, I swim along the shore against the current and then have an easy ride back. I change into dry trunks near the dune. Except on big weekends, there is no one there to object as I do my Dance of the Seven Veils, and even on big weekends no one does. Back home, I'd try to work until I felt hungry. That was the signal to drive to the Sagaponack post office. Because it's more pleasant to do business there than in

Bridgehampton, I rent a box in Sagaponack, gladly paying a nonresident's fee. At Loaves & Fishes at the intersection of Sagg Main and Route 27, I'd pick up a salad for my lunch and perhaps a couple of slices of roast beef for my dinner. I'd stop at the farm stand a few hundred yards up the road, hoping that the young woman I call the girl with the golden skin will be on duty, and buy lettuce, tomatoes—the best in the world—and fruit. If setting out my food on the kitchen table felt like a bore, I'd drive from the post office straight to Candy Kitchen, a luncheonette in Bridgehampton, and have my midday meal there. Always the same, eaten at the counter: smoked salmon on whole wheat toast and innumerable cups of black coffee. The balletic activity of the Greek family working at the place, and a peek at the headlines, which I usually find amusing, on front pages of the *Post* and the *Daily News,* on display along with the *Times,* the *Wall Street Journal,* the *Financial Times,* and the local press, were all the entertainment I wanted or needed.

Once or twice a week—always on a weekday—I'd go to dinner at the American Hotel in Sag Harbor, arriving late, when the noise level was usually lower. And that was it. Most of my old Hampton pals had died during the last ten years. One has moved away, to be near a son who lives in New Hampshire. A classmate is sinking into dementia. Yup. *The thinning of our ranks each year / Affords a hint we are nigh undone, / That we shall not be ever again / The marked of many, loved of one* ... I didn't let the remaining three or four friends more or less my age, or the scattering of the younger people I like, know that I was spending the summer in Bridgehampton. Why? Valerie was the principal reason. I didn't want to hear what they had to say about her having dumped me: neither expressions of sympathy with me nor hostile remarks directed at her. That I was trying to work hard was another justification. The strongest, the real reason, though, was that everyone I would have truly liked to see was among the pals who were dead. The work progressed, without bringing me much satisfaction. Daily I wondered whether I shouldn't simply drop it. But I kept typing, and when I'd done a number of pages I considered sufficient for the day, I'd have a nap or do some laps in the swimming pool. Afterward, I'd get quietly crocked. Philip Larkin hit the nail on the head when he said: *I work all day, and get half-drunk at night.* I don't hold liquor so well as I used to, so a couple of stiff drinks of bourbon with barely an ice cube or a vodka out of the freezer and a couple of glasses of wine taken with my dinner were enough to get me there.

My children were maintaining a silence that at first only puzzled me, and by and by began to offend me. To be sure, I had told them long ago that there was no need to call me on any sort of schedule—a daily call had been something my father had insisted on after my mother died, Please call to make sure I'm still alive was his obnoxious line—and that I despised robotic gestures and expressions. For instance, when my daughter, Barbara, at one point began to sign off at the end of her telephone conversations with *Love ya,* I ruthlessly repressed that tic. My own line was: Call me when you have something you want to say or something you want to ask. It turned out that Barbara and Roddy had no trouble absorbing that "don't feel you need to check on the old man" precept. As for me, I became accustomed to their calling rarely, usually as part of their multitasking—when driving along a boring stretch of the road or watching the evening news, which I could hear in the background. Barbara's calls, the ones timed for when I would have finished breakfast but hadn't yet gone out, were often of the "I've something I'd sort of like to ask you" variety. Duly translated, they meant: I want some money. For the kids' piano and dance lessons, summer camp fees, and the like. Why her dermatologist husband, practicing in Wellesley, which is, to my knowledge, still a wealthy suburb, can't afford that stuff, I don't know. The truth is that I don't much care. When I am invited, for instance, to fund my elder granddaughter Trudy's first-year tuition at a private day school, a sum for which I could have bought for myself a Mercedes two-seater, I reply, But of course. Why should I say no? I have no desire to become the owner of that two-seater and I love unconditionally my daughter and granddaughters. Somewhat to my surprise, Roddy has not yet conducted a serious raid on my bank account. He is doing well at his not-quite-top-tier law firm, but I don't think that is the reason. More likely it is the availability of satisfactory public schools in Chappaqua, where they reside half a mile up the road from the Clintons. I have only had to pay for his twin boys' summer camp and similar trifles. My annoyance at their neglecting me, I have to confess, grew whenever I recalled Barbara's and Rod's telephone communications with their mother. In Barbara's case, they had been frequent and lengthy. As one might expect from a working lawyer, Rod called less often and didn't stay on the phone for more than fifteen, twenty minutes at a time. But his wife, Carla, a Dutch graduate student he met at Harvard Law School, a good-natured massive blonde with about as much charm as a chunk of Gouda cheese, took up the slack.

Why were the children ignoring me? Fundamental indifference to my welfare? An aggressive expression of loyalty to their mother that was really misplaced, since it was she who left me for another man with whom she'd been cheating on me for some time, and, because I'm a patsy, was getting all she wanted under the separation agreement? She didn't really claim I'd wronged her; when you came right down to it, all she claimed was that she couldn't stand me. The real reason she dumped me was that she had fallen for that much-younger man. A good-looking guy, I was forced to admit, having Googled him and examined the photos. Had my children some other grievance I couldn't think of? It occurred to me that probably I wasn't much fun to talk to. Perhaps they too had come to dislike me. It was sad but didn't really matter. Nor did the more general void around me. Even before Valerie left, I hardly ever went out to lunch (occasional lunches at my club didn't enter into my calculations). There were fewer and fewer people whose dinner parties I enjoyed. As for the dinners Valerie gave at home with such élan, well, they were her dinners and therefore just fine with me. There was no mystery about that. The sad truth is that I had loved her and rejoiced in everything that gave her pleasure. Her absence, her not being there, was painful beyond anything I had imagined. I think I missed her most in bed. Not so much because I wanted sex—perhaps her departure had accelerated the dwindling of my libido—but because I craved the contact with her warm body.

My beautiful house in Bridgehampton was maintained by Gloria the housekeeper, Gus the pool man, Ricardo the gardener, Jeremiah the handyman, and Sam the house watcher. Nice people, who knew they had a good deal with me, and took in calmly the news that Valerie wouldn't be around—anyway, not with me, but the Hamptons being the Hamptons I supposed they could envisage her return to the neighborhood as the companion of another, richer man, and, as such, a replacement employer and source of revenue. So could the tactful owners and the help at the fruit stand, Loaves & Fishes, Candy Kitchen, and the hardware store. I wondered how it would go in the city. There were two other apartments on my floor. The tenant owners and I exchanged cheery greetings in the elevator, but I had no other contact with them. Valerie was on a first-name basis with the wives—perhaps the husbands as well—knew the schools the children attended, who worked where, and so forth. None of these neighbors had commented to me on her disappearance. She must have given them a heads-up. And just what had she told them? The building's personnel—the elevator men, the doormen, the rear-elevator men, the handyman, and the live-in building manager—that was another matter. I was well aware of the minute scrutiny to which they subjected the tenants' lives and the ups and downs in their fortunes. I thought they were well disposed toward me, if only because I was a generous tipper. Some of them even slapped me occasionally on the shoulder, a supremely friendly gesture that would have caused my father to have them fired. What had they been saying behind our backs before Valerie left, and what were they saying now that she had walked out on that nice Mr. G.? I was ready to bet dollars to donuts that they knew more than I about my marriage and what had gone wrong in it. Naturally, they too made no comment.

One day in August it rained so hard that I decided against going to the post office or to Candy Kitchen. Staying in my office, and pretending to work, in reality I waited impatiently for Gloria to leave. I was hungry. She'd come in to ask whether she should set the table for my lunch, but I told her not to bother, I was going to have a bite in Sag Harbor. I really didn't want her to offer to stay to wash the salad or do the dishes or whatever good action might come into her head, and above all I didn't want to hear her say she was sorry I'd be having lunch alone. As soon as she was gone, I set the table myself, in the kitchen rather than in the dining room, scrambled four eggs, and washed them down with a half bottle of Italian red. A fellow must keep his strength up in bad weather was what my father used to say, and, after

I'd had my coffee and put away the dishes, I went upstairs to take a nap. To hell with working. After all, I wasn't on a deadline. It was luxuriously pleasant to stretch out on the bed and enter the land that lies at the border between thought and dream. As I lingered there, a project took form in my head. It was to bring under my roof another living being—only it wouldn't be a live-in cook or a girlfriend. It would be a nice dog. My experience with dogs was limited. The dachshunds my parents had kept and doted on would snap at me when I was little, and a couple of times even drew blood. As I grew bigger, they took to ignoring me. But they hadn't turned me against all dogs, only that breed. There was a very fine dog I knew, a French bulldog called Hugo, yes, my own name, which could be a favorable omen, belonging to my second cousin once removed, Sally Porter, a glamorous Southampton divorcée, at fifty-seven or -eight successfully hanging on to her very good looks. Her Hugo had taken a shine to me, jumping into my lap the first time I met him, when Valerie and I went to Sally's for dinner. I had fallen for him too. I had a cup of coffee, called Sally, and asked where I could get a Frenchie just like Hugo.

At the pet store, she told me.

I laughed, and said, You've become a real comic.

It was her turn to chortle. No, I'm not joking. It's not how much is that doggy in the window, the one with the waggly tail. After Jodie died—that was her aged fox terrier, whom I'd also known and liked—I asked the vet to recommend a breeder of Frenchies. For some reason, I'd decided that's what I wanted. Probably because they're so different from my lovely Jodie.

Don't go to a breeder, he said, they'll give you the puppy they want to sell just then, and not necessarily the one you want. You won't have any choice. With them, it's that puppy or nothing. Go to a pet store I'll give you the name and address of the one you should visit. They have the best animals, and you can play with the puppies and decide which one you really like. If they don't have a Frenchie right now, they'll tell you when one or two will be coming in.

So that's what I did, she continued. If you want to talk to the vet he'll be glad to advise you. He's a nice man.

I don't think I need to, I told her, your recommendation is good enough. I'll call the store, and if they have a candidate I'll go into the city and look him or her over.

Do, she answered, and when you have your Frenchie, you and Valerie must bring him over for a playdate.

You have a deal, but it will have to be just the puppy and me, I told her. Valerie and I have split. We've signed a separation agreement and we're waiting for the divorce to come through. There is no reason why you should have heard. Perhaps I should have told you.

That's so too bad. Was this your idea?

Entirely hers. She's got a guy. A Frenchman who owns or runs a restaurant in Chelsea. She sprung it on me some months ago. I had no idea that he existed.

She's an idiot. Buy your dog and both of you come to dinner. You'll be surprised at how good a divorce can make you feel—after a while!

I thanked her and said both the advice and the invitation were gratefully accepted.

The next morning, I called the pet store. They had three French bulldog puppies who were, as the man I spoke to put it, ready to go. I drove to the city, put the car in a garage, and feeling nervous and expectant walked four blocks to the shop. Yes, the Frenchies were there, two of them tan and one black and white. He was bigger and wider across the chest than his crate mates.

He's a boy, the salesman explained, the two other puppies are girls. Also, he's almost six months old. They're just three. Here, I'll put him on the counter, so you can pet him.

The Frenchie remained in place for a split second. A leap with the liftoff power of a rocket carried him into my arms, from which position he began licking my face.

I guess he likes you, Mr. Gardner, observed the salesman.

Laughing too hard to answer, I only nodded my head.

When the puppy calmed himself, I asked the salesman why, in his opinion, this little dog was for sale at such an advanced age.

I don't know, he replied. It could be because he's expensive. It could be because the breeder had a buyer for him and the buyer backed out. He'd forfeit his deposit, of course, but that does happen. People's circumstances change. But he's a good puppy, and he's already paper trained.

Meanwhile the puppy was making noises in my arms the likes of which I had never heard, somewhere between a gurgle and a snort. Gazing at me steadfastly out of huge protruding black eyes set in shiny white corneas, he communicated, I thought, just a touch of impatience. What are you waiting for, you old idiot? Can't you tell you and I are meant to be together?

I'll buy him, I told the salesman, and I'd like to take him with me. My car is four blocks away. I can be here in ten, fifteen minutes. If I drive by, will you have him ready?

That turned out to be what not only the puppy but also the salesman expected, but first came the paperwork. Because the puppy was a high-bred aristocrat, his new abode had to be duly registered, and a great deal of advice given about diet, vaccinations, and also the first visit to the vet, to take place as soon as possible. If the vet found the puppy was unsound, I could return him. It occurred to me that it would take a very grave problem to induce me to do that.

And what will be his name? the salesman asked. Have you thought of one? Louis is a popular name for Frenchies. You can send me an email when you decide.

But I did have one. It had come to me in a flash: Sam.

A good name, said the salesman. We need time to complete all the formalities, so if you haven't eaten by all means go to lunch and pick Sam up after your meal.

My club was closed for the summer vacation. Members could use the dining room of two clubs in the vicinity of Bloomingdale's, but I was too nervous to think seriously of sitting down to a real lunch, especially at a place where, heaven forfend, I might be obliged to enter into a conversation with strangers. I stumbled on a luncheonette crowded with shoppers already in possession of big brown bags and had a smoked-salmon sandwich and a double espresso. I knew nothing about French bulldogs other than that I liked a lot the looks and personality of Sally's Hugo, the only Frenchie I knew. My iPhone was fully charged, and I decided to Google the breed. Athletic, playful, and headstrong, I learned; brachycephalic and therefore highly sensitive to hot weather and cold; unable to swim because of body weight in relation to legs and, again, because they are brachycephalic. All this was fine. Longevity: ten to fourteen years. I shrugged, realizing that I had no idea what the life expectancy might be of Labradors or poodles, to take breeds I was accustomed to seeing. And then, suddenly, a devastating thought came into my head: in the natural course of events, Sam was bound to outlive me. I was about to bring into my house a marvelous little animal who would learn to love me even as I loved him, the bond of affection between us strengthening with the passage of each day, and then, after a few good years, I would leave him. Orphaned with no place to go, no roof over his head other than some animal rescue center! Would Barbara take him in? Certainly not Barbara; she had I didn't know how many cats. And Rod? He had always disliked dogs. I had no business exposing this little Frenchie to such a future. It would be the equivalent of having children when you're so old that you know that statistically you're near certain not to be around to bring them up. Like Eddie Sharp, my recently deceased prep-school roommate! At the age of sixty plus the old fool married a woman half his age, and, in the space of two years, he gave her two children. Ten years later, a stroke left him paralyzed from the waist down. As some classmates less fond of him than I like to quip, he timed it so that soon the kids would be big enough to push him to Central Park in his wheelchair. I knew that right-thinking people would say that Eddie and his wife, Kitty, and their children were people, while the Frenchie was just a puppy in a Lexington Avenue pet store waiting for a buyer, but that sensible distinction didn't ease my mind. I called for the check, paid, and dragged myself back to the store.

I can't take the puppy, I told the salesman. I'm horribly sorry. I apologize to you and to him. If there is a breakup fee due at this point, I will of course pay it. But I can't take him. I just can't.

Why? asked the salesman, sounding as incredulous as he looked. You really like him. He really likes you. Is it the price?

No, I replied, certainly not. It's my age and his longevity. I'm eighty-four and I live alone. I looked up his longevity as I was having lunch. It's ten, fourteen years. I don't want to leave an orphan.

But you look very fit, sir, and if the worst happened, I'm sure a friend would take this wonderful little dog.

Perhaps. But I can't let him run the risk.

I had two hundred dollars in fifties ready in my pocket and gave them to the man. He made a show of protesting, then took the money, thanked me, and said, If you ever change your mind...

I drove to Bridgehampton feeling hollowed out and sadder than at any time since the day I was told that Valerie was leaving me. I'd borrowed an audio book of *A Handful of Dust* from the Bridgehampton library for the trip home, thinking that I might need something livelier to keep me awake than whatever was happening on the Metropolitan Opera Sirius channel. The traffic thickened around LaGuardia. While the car was momentarily stopped, I slipped the first CD into the reader. The book made me even sadder, if that was possible. I couldn't help taking personally the way Brenda Last dumped the thickheaded, unsuspecting Tony, and banged my fist on the steering wheel in protest against each new piece of cruel perversity. Poor Tony had no one. Absolutely no one. Just like me, since I was beginning to think that Barbara and Rod didn't count. But it didn't have to be that way. If I had taken the little French bulldog home with me, if I hadn't made another huge mistake, one of so many that littered my life, I would have had him in my corner. It would have been hard cheese on all the Brendas in the world.

Why had I let those idiotic scruples possess me? The little puppy wasn't some trust beneficiary with a bright future ahead of him that I was about to put at risk. He was a little dog who at six months old had failed to sell and was sitting in a crate in a pet store on Lexington Avenue. Who was to tell when he would be sold and to whom? And what if he didn't sell in a week, two weeks, three weeks? Would the price go down so radically that a buyer was bound to appear? But what if there was no buyer, what happened then? And who was to say that a buyer who ultimately materialized would give the little Frenchie a good life? I remembered that friends who have dogs often made it a point of honor that they had gotten from a shelter a rescue animal, an animal no one wanted, that faced the bleak future of euthanasia. By taking one of those dogs, they weren't feeding, they'd say, the puppy mill industry, dogs being bred in ever-larger numbers to satisfy the whims of buyers. All right, I understood that, but wasn't Sam the equivalent of a rescue dog, a dog I had no part in causing to be brought to life, who was there alive and yearning for a home? What in the Lord's name had gotten into me? Why had I done this to him and to myself?

III

T HE SUMMER OF 2015 and the impulsive decision
not to take the little Frenchie home with me were
long past, but regret over Sam persisted. It persisted even though I no longer had any doubt that I had
made the right decision. Not only because the puppy would
almost surely outlive me, and be left an orphan, but because
of the way I lived. If I went out of the house, for however long
that might be, the puppy would be absolutely alone, unless
my housekeeper happened to be there. What right had I to
keep the little puppy prisoner—in solitary confinement—for
hours and hours so that I might enjoy his company when it
suited me to come home? I had no answer to that question.
Certainly, the fact that dogs all over the city suffered exactly
that fate while their owners were at the office, the dogs' solitude interrupted only by visits of a dog walker, was not an
adequate rejoinder.

Having accepted Mark Horowitz's invitation that had come

so handily on the heels of the divorce decree, I went to his party. Ted Cruz announced his candidacy that very day. That anyone so egregiously mean and evil looking could aspire to be the president of the United States was hard to believe, but there he was before our eyes. Joe McCarthy redux. The consensus of Mark's guests was that Hillary would make mincemeat of him. If there were Republicans among us, they kept their mouths shut. I did too. My little book on Bill's presidency had marked me as a Clinton hater. I didn't want to pour oil on the fire by pointing out that she was herself an unattractive candidate and was unlikely to make mincemeat of anybody. Of course, that didn't mean that I would vote for any of the other lamentable Republicans who appeared likely to emerge. I knew I'd vote for Hillary because I don't believe in abstentions, and, in the end, I did, holding my nose. How could she have been so mercenary? Extracting those outrageous fees for speeches to Goldman Sachs bankers on the eve of a presidential campaign she and Bill knew she would undertake, and then be stupid and maladroit enough to refuse to release the text of those speeches—for what reason? Was their banality so embarrassing? Had she made outrageous promises to her audiences? Perhaps she really had. It would figure. After all, we owed to Bill the deregulation of financial institutions and its dire consequences. Neither the interminable cocktail hour nor the dinner—spaghetti and meatballs to be eaten off a plate balanced on one's knees and chocolate cake that was too sweet for my taste—improved my mood. I knew most of the guests and noted that they had aged by at least ten years since I last saw them. Several were in worse shape than I, leaning on canes, supported by their spouses when they helped themselves at the buffet table. One colleague, who had been in Moscow for the *Wall Street Journal* at the same time as I, was using a walker. He noticed my surprise and told me he'd had a back operation. Fused disks, he added. It's a lousy procedure, don't let them do it to you. Yet they were all apparently having a fine time, even the Republicans if any were present. As for me, I wished I had not left the orderly quiet of my kitchen where I could have treated myself to scrambled eggs and better wine than Mark's California Merlot.

I did drive out to Bridgehampton the following Friday morning, and, as promised, went to Penny's dinner on Saturday. Distrusting my memory or steadiness of purpose, she had called twice during the week to make sure of it, repeating the directions to her house. The second time she called, it occurred to me that Valerie might have spread the rumor that I had Alzheimer's or something like it. She might have thought it was a better reason for leaving me than Monsieur Leblanc and his Chelsea bistro. I didn't say that to Penny and instead asked whether she thought I was losing my mind. How could she have forgotten the countless times I had driven to her house in Springs from my house in Bridgehampton.

Oh no, chirped Penny, it's just that I've always assumed that Valerie was your navigator.

———

But before Penny's Saturday dinner, on Wednesday of that week I saw my daughter, Barbara, for the first time since an afternoon a couple of weeks before Christmas. She called on Tuesday and said, I'm coming to the city tomorrow morning. It's Mom's birthday, you know.

I told her I knew.

Indeed, it was an occasion I had used to make sure we celebrated with great verve at a family lunch, usually on the Sunday before the actual date, so that the grandchildren could participate.

Yes, she continued, but we're doing it on the right date, at Louis's bistro.

Perhaps I had become dim. It took me a moment to realize that Louis was the lucky restaurateur.

She continued, while I put my thoughts in order: Randy (that was the dermatologist husband) can't make it, but Roddy and Carla (my Dutch daughter-in-law) are on. Thank God, no children! Anyway, can we have lunch or something?

Certainly, I replied. Any particular place? Would you like to have lunch here, at home? Would you like to stay with me, at home?

No, that wouldn't work. How about lunch at your club? It's convenient to the subway.

Aha, I thought, she's staying with *maman* and *beau-papa* or *beau-papa*-to-be. Are nuptials a part of the plan? So far, no one had bothered to tell me.

Certainly, I replied again. Any particular hour?

Twelve, twelve-fifteen.

It was a few minutes past twelve-thirty when she showed up, looking dowdy, I thought, in a gray woolen skirt that was too long and a gray cardigan.

Train was late, she announced.

I had been waiting for her upstairs, nursing a Virgin Mary, and asked whether she would like to have a drink first or go directly up to lunch.

Let's have lunch, if you don't mind. Perhaps I can have a glass of wine with the food.

She ate with gusto, drank her glass of Pinot Noir, and asked for another, and told me about the developments in her husband's practice, principally his offering a new cryogenic method for removing unwanted fat (love handles, double chins, and the like), Trudy's progress at her school where she was now in the eighth grade, and her sister Emma's having been accepted for admission in the fall by the kindergarten that Trudy had attended. This turned out to be the preface to a "by the way, Dad, the schools have each asked for a deposit." She handed me an envelope and said, The bills are inside. Do you think you could send your check directly to the admissions office?

I wasn't going to spoil the meal by asking what was the matter with the dermatologist's checkbook, or offering some other witticism, so I simply said, Certainly, congratulations to Emma.

It really didn't matter. That was the conclusion I had come

to and I would stick to it. I had enough money, I was sure, to live out my life in comfort, even if it dragged on, even if live-in help was required. Either the house in Bridgehampton or the apartment in the city would have to be sold—I could foresee that keeping the two places would become a burden financially and otherwise—reducing considerably my fixed expenses. Really, handing over those checks to Barbara or Rod when he decided to get on the gravy train as a matter of distributive justice, if not actual need, only meant that when I died (the sooner the better, I was coming to think, however much I liked this vale of tears) there would be less money for them and their children. That was not something I was going to worry about, and I certainly wouldn't reduce, on their account, my bequests to Harvard College and my prep school.

I saw that she had nothing of note to say to me, now that the school deposit check had been promised, and decided to risk talking about Valerie.

You probably haven't thought about it, I said, but your mother's affair with Mr. Louis Lenoir...

Cut it out, Dad, she interrupted. It's Leblanc.

Sorry, her affair with Monsieur whatever his name is. That fact, and her decision to ask for a divorce, took me totally by surprise. Forgive me for asking, but did you know about the affair? Did you know that she was sleeping with this guy and was as unhappy with me as she and her lawyer alleged? I had been quite sure that we had a good marriage. That's what I would have said if anyone had asked me.

Are you serious? No, you've got to be kidding.

I am serious. We had lived quietly and comfortably, both here and in the country, your mother's work and career were exactly on track, I've been scribbling, minding my own business, so really, what is the elephant or rhinoceros in the room that I failed to see? I had an appointment with my doctor a couple of weeks ago, and we had a very long talk. If he had noticed signs of my losing my mind, not knowing what goes on around me, I'm sure he would have said so, or sent me to see a neurologist.

You're really hopeless, Dad. No one says you're demented. You're just unbearably dreary and unbearably selfish. And old! I know you're eighty-four or eighty-five, but you act as though you were one hundred. As though you were dead. A walking corpse! You don't want to do anything, you don't want to go anywhere, you don't want to see anyone! All right. If Mom organized a dinner at home, you'd get the wine out and sit at the head of the table and make your usual unpleasant remarks. Same deal when she dragged you to a dinner. Mr. Hugo Gardner in his Saville Row suit, Charvet shirt and Charvet tie, not a piece of the equipment out of place, trots along with her, makes same sort of stupid remarks, and can't wait to go home. And Dad, the way you look! You should have had those bags under your eyes fixed ten, fifteen years ago, and get rid of all those liver or God knows what they are spots on your face. You look horrible. Mom is still young and beautiful and needs to live, to have fun. Maybe if you knew Louis you'd understand that when he made his moves she realized right away that was what she wanted. What she needed!

She stopped. I guessed she had come to the end of her speech and asked whether she'd like another glass of wine and dessert.

Yes, to both.

While one waiter poured the wine, and another wheeled over the dessert cart—she chose the fruit salad—I contemplated her. Thirty-six. Very pretty. Looks like her mother. Speaking of bags under eyes, systems of wrinkles were forming under hers. Ditto for corners of her mouth. No lipstick, of course, not sure about powder.

Well, I said, you've certainly opened my eyes. In your memory as a young girl and a young adult, was I always as awful?

It's a stupid question, Dad. Mom brought us up. You were always traveling on assignment or working till midnight or whatever. I feel I hardly knew you.

There is something to what you said. My work was very absorbing. That's what happens when you're a foreign correspondent and then a bureau chief and so on. Now another stupid question. Are your mother and Monsieur Leblanc planning to get married now that she is officially divorced?

Yes. This summer, when the restaurant closes for a month. Anything else about their life together you need to know?

Nothing about your mother's life with Monsieur Leblanc. I hope it's as happy as she hoped. But I'm curious about your daughters. I haven't seen them since your mother left. Not in the country, where you used to visit, not at Thanksgiving or Christmas, to which you used to invite us. The reason?

Mom would have flipped if I'd gone to stay with you in Bridgehampton. Both she and Louis were with us, in Wellesley, for Thanksgiving and Christmas. We didn't think you'd fit in.

That's what I was beginning to think. Now I have an unrelated and final question. Why have you asked to see me? Only to extract the checks for school deposits? Any other reason?

I really hate you, Dad, she answered. And now I'm leaving.

Do, I said. I think you can find your way out. I want to have a cup of coffee.

It seemed only fair to give my son, Rod, an equal chance to berate me. I called from downstairs at the club to make an appointment and to my surprise found that he was free for lunch the next day. Things were slow at the office, he said. Partners were going around saying they'd kill for a deal.

At the club? I asked. At twelve-thirty or one or some hour in the middle, as you like.

One o'clock. I'll see you there.

I had some time ago arranged for him to be put up for the club, and he was recently elected, a small accomplishment that gave me considerable pleasure. I liked meeting him there for lunch. It reminded me of my father's satisfaction when I became a member and how proud he was, the few times we attended the members' monthly dinner and meeting together, to introduce me as "my boy Hugo" to other aged relics gathered there who were his friends. That business at Rod's firm should be slow troubled me. What was the impact on his income? I did not believe that the firm was one of the strongest in the city. Partners' compensation there was a function of the business they brought in and handled, not as in some of the very top firms that are on what they call the lockstep system, with all partners of the same seniority being paid the same unless some sort of punitive action is taken against a screwup. If the level of Rod's workload was low, his compensation would probably be reduced according to some system administered by the management. How much impact would that have on his standard of living? He'd done well, but no better than that, at Harvard College and Harvard Law School. No honors at either place. He had standard WASP good looks; he was well mannered, well dressed, serious, and agreeable. In my day, considering his background, that would most probably have been enough to get him first a summer job between his second and third years of law school and then, after the third year, a permanent position at one of the great Wall Street firms. The fact that my father had been a leading partner at Morgan Stanley and that I ran *Time*, a position generally considered one of influence if not power, would not have been disregarded. Or a more distant connection: a direct ancestor on my mother's side had commanded a Union brigade in the Battle of Bull Run. "Background" did not seem to weigh in the scales held by these more modern hiring partners. They passed on him. Fair or not, it was too bad for Rod.

He arrived at one on the dot. I observed with pleasure that his suit fit well, that his necktie was just right, and that he had a nice tan.

You've been in the sun, I remarked after we'd settled down at a table in the members' dining room.

Yes, he said, didn't Carla tell you? We went to Palm Beach with the children over the Martin Luther King weekend and had very good weather. I played a lot of tennis.

That's very nice, I said. I'm sure it did all of you a world of good.

He nodded energetically.

We studied the menu, filled out our lunch order chits, and sat back. After the waiter had collected them and poured glasses of red wine we had ordered, I decided to put the question to him.

Rod, I said, you've mentioned business at the firm being slow. Is this something one should worry about?

Yes and no, he answered. It's always better if the demand is growing and the firm is working at full tilt. It makes the boys and girls happy. But the slowness is a general phenomenon in the city, not just us, and it was worse last year. We're worried but not really worried.

Well, that's good. First good news I've heard in a long time.

We were silent while the waiter brought Rod's clams on

the half shell and my fisherman soup. That out of the way, I said, You won't be surprised, Rod, to learn that I wanted to speak to you about your mother. Her departure—the speed, the reasons, I mean both the accusations she has leveled at me and the appearance of Monsieur Leblanc, whose existence I had ignored—have knocked me for a loop. I understand it was no surprise to you. In fact, you referred your mother to Mr. Sweeney. And it wasn't a surprise to Barbara. By the way, I had lunch with her yesterday.

Yes, I know, Rod muttered. I saw her at Mom's birthday yesterday evening.

Precisely. I found out that was the reason she had come down to New York. Why she wanted to see me is another story. It may seem odd to you that I'm going to try to talk to you about your mother and Monsieur Leblanc only now that the divorce has come through. I've no experience in such matters, but I can't help thinking that in most families there would have been conversations between the children and the parent who is being as it were left behind. But neither you nor Barbara seemed to want a conversation and, quite frankly, I was so surprised and so shocked by what had happened that I felt shy? reluctant? ashamed? to talk about it. What has changed? For one thing, the divorce is final, and I feel the need for a backward glance. Not as part of moving on, because I'm not at all sure that moving on, whatever that means, is in the cards for me. It's just a need. Then yesterday Barbara—what shall I say?—gave me a piece of her mind. Perhaps that's not the right way to put it. Painted a picture of me that's so repulsive that your mother's decision to leave me, with or without Monsieur Leblanc, seems practically inevitable. Really, I had never suspected I was so awful.

Rod raised his hand.

Dad, Dad, he said, cool it. Barbara is batty—about this anyway. She's gone way over the top. That's Carla's opinion too. Barbara thinks she has a God-given mission: to defend Mom against any criticism. If that means demolishing you, so be it. Why that is, I can't be sure. Carla isn't either and she has talked to Barbara a lot. Believe me, a lot!

May I be pompous for just a moment and tell you that it's truly kind of you to have said this? But if you don't think I'm quite the monster that Barbara claims I am, in your opinion what did happen? After such a long time of being married and living together comfortably and peacefully? At least that is something that should be next to impossible to deny.

What happened? It's not that complicated, Dad. You're going to be eighty-five this year, Mom has just turned sixty-three, Louis Leblanc is even younger than Mom—by the way I hope that doesn't turn out to be a problem for them. He put the make on her and he's a handsome and, I can well imagine, sexy dude. Apparently very successful in his business, which, don't forget, is in a way Mom's business too. He owns a second restaurant in Brooklyn and another in Paris, somewhere in the *cinquième*. Put it together, and it doesn't seem a big mystery.

I guess not, I replied, and suggested we have another glass of wine.

Rod glanced at his watch and said, Let's do it. I'll have two espressos and walk back to the office and hope I can stay awake at the ballet. I'm meeting Carla, he added. There's an all-Balanchine program at the City Ballet she wants to see.

That's very nice. Your mother would probably be glad to join you. With Monsieur Leblanc!

Now, Dad! Louis works evenings and she's at the stage of going out without him only for professional reasons. She'll get over it.

Doubtless, I said. I have a confession to make. Being old, really old like me, isn't any fun. I have no reason not to go to the ballet tonight or any night next week. I'm just not going. It's true I'm going to the opera tomorrow. *Così fan tutte*. Ha! Ha! Ha!

In vino veritas, Dad. I'll add two things to what we've been talking about. First, by way of further explanation of Mom's departure. I don't know whether it's a necessary consequence of getting to be your age, but it's a fact that for a number of years now living with you can't have been much fun—perhaps any fun. You've been behind your desk most of the time working on a book. All right. That's understandable. Mom worked too on her TV show, her articles, and so forth. But the idea of going to the theater or a concert or the ballet—that didn't seem to occur to you anymore. Big change. Only the opera, because of your sacrosanct subscription. And you don't want to travel. You! A renowned foreign correspondent! Paris, no. Everybody you knew there is dead or in the last stage of dotage. Venice, no. Too many tourists, you've been there too often. Plus, a variant on the everyone-is-dead theme: all the restaurant owners and headwaiters you knew have retired. But have Titian and Veronese retired? No, you say, but how many times do I need to see the paintings that are already imprinted in my memory? Another thing: Mom says you find everyone boring. Your old friends, new people, everybody. A sort of weird shrinking of your interests.

I couldn't help it. I was laughing. You're right, I said. Exactly right.

I know I'm right, Dad. I've been studying you. Now a further gloss on Barbs. You know that I've never been in analysis and I've never much liked amateur analysts. But I have been slowly building a theory about Barbara. It's that her excessive—hysterical—need not only to justify Mom's departure but also to demolish you has something to do with her evolving attitude toward her husband. She's taken to saying very nasty things about poor old Randy. He may be the greatest dermatologist in Wellesley, who knows, maybe even in Boston, but he's the biggest bore. A terminal case. If Barbara consciously or subconsciously is planning to leave him to his cryogenic fat-removal machine and bodybuilding—you do know that's what he does—it might make sense to demonstrate to her own satisfaction and the satisfaction of whoever she can get to listen that there is rock-solid precedent for such a move for such a reason. Her own mom didn't hesitate to do it.

Cripes, Roddy! Do you think she has someone, her own Monsieur Lenoir or Leblanc?

That's a question Carla and I have put to ourselves. We don't know. There hasn't been any mention of such a person. But who can tell? A suburban wife, husband all day at the office or lifting weights at the gym, the kids at school, she is the right age...

Well, I said, if she does anything of the sort, she had better get a hell of a settlement from old Randy or fly into the arms of someone with a big bank account and a generous disposition. She has no profession, no qualifications, she has never worked, she's been supported by Randy with some handouts from me. That's all! I begged her to go to graduate school before getting married to Randy and settling down in Wellesley. No, she'd had it with school, even courses at the School of Education that would have qualified her to teach kindergarten or early grades. I begged her to take courses at the Harvard Division of Continuing Education once she settled down in Wellesley, something that could be fitted into any housewife's schedule. No. Too inconvenient. Roddy, she's never worked.

Well, she did coach tennis summers.

At the Wellesley Country Club! Really, Rod!

Now, Dad, get the snob inside you under control. Sure, she wasn't coaching at Myopia, but, apparently, she did a good job and she was a hell of a good player.

All right, all right, the Wellesley club is a great institution if you want to meet dermatologists, insurance brokers, and bank vice presidents. And she was a good player. Used to cream me. But I don't think her future lies in tennis, and she had better be careful.

Agreed. He looked at his watch again. It's time for that trek back to the office. It was good to see you, Dad.

I stood up and, contrary to our habit, embraced him.

I too felt the need of a walk. In my case, I walked home, up Park Avenue. On an impulse, I stopped at Sherry-Lehmann, where I'd been buying wine since I came back to New York City after the army and settled down in a little apartment of my own. Only that was before the great wine merchants' merger; at the time I dealt with Mr. Lehmann. A small gesture of independence, since my father dealt with Sherry? My trusted and unfailingly well-informed saleslady was at the shop, but on the telephone. I waited until she got off, and guided by her I sent Rod a case of Cheval Blanc '61. I made a face at the thought of sending him a Saint-Émillion—I'm a Pomerol and Saint-Estèphe man—but she said, You won't regret it, Mr. Gardner.

If you have an adviser you trust, you better follow her advice. Advice, I might add, that was instantly validated by the huge price of the case.

Done! I said.

On the card to go with the wine I wrote: You're a good guy, Roddy! We should have lunch more often.

IV

UCH AS I LIKED PENNY LUDINGTON, I disliked the drive from my house on Bridge Lane to her place in Springs. In the summer, which now seems to begin in the Hamptons on Memorial Day weekend, the traffic on Route 27 going east is appalling, particularly on Friday and Saturday evenings, while Route 114, which I can pick up in Sag Harbor and stay on until East Hampton, is plain dangerous on weekends. Too many drivers speeding—or speeding and drunk. Nevertheless, that is the route I normally take going to Penny's, hitting Route 27 at the last possible moment. Coming home at night after dinner I stay on Route 27 all the way. At least it's clearly marked, with a good solid yellow line down the middle. These tiresome considerations were part of the reason for my lack of enthusiasm as I shaved and otherwise got ready to go to dinner and reflected on how pleasant it would be to sit down in my kitchen to a meal of hot beef bouillon, bread, cheese, dry sausage, and an apple. The weightier reason was the one that made me wince when Roddy put his finger on it: the shrinking of my interests. The unpleasant discovery that old friends, new people, really practically everybody bores me. Exempted are people, usually younger than my children, I meet and take a fancy to. Sometimes, a fleeting fancy. It can be a new librarian at the Society Library, my internist's truly charming and efficient secretary, a young lawyer from Larry Weinstein's office who gave me a hand with the dreary business of handing over to Valerie's counsel Sweeney the stuff they took off my walls and out of the cabinets in which the glass and pâté de verre pieces I gave her were displayed, a young woman with skin the color of old gold and gleaming white teeth who was studying to be a dental hygienist and in the summer helped out at the fruit-and-vegetable stand, the one I called the girl with the golden skin. These younger creatures, whom I do my best to engage in conversation, give me the impression that a door is opening on unfamiliar worlds and lives the outlines of which I could not otherwise discover. As for Penny—she is in a category all her own. She almost became my girlfriend when I was a senior at Harvard College and she in her first year at Radcliffe. The prospect of spending an evening with her gave me pleasure. But her guests... I think I could guess who they would be. An investment banker who had been our ambassador to Turkey during George W.'s first term. I guessed he'd agree if pressed that his boss's tenure had been disastrous, but, so far, we had stayed off that subject. His wife, who was on the board of the Museum of the City of New York and asked each time we saw each other whether I had known Louis Auchincloss. A couple, both painters, the wife rather better than the husband. A retired gay real-estate broker of good family with a pretty house on Union Street in Sag Harbor and, if we were lucky, Penny's gay sinologist nephew.

I wouldn't have minded living in Penny's house itself once I got there. A large brown-shingled structure that had been added to over the last one hundred years or more, it was in perfect contrast with my prim little home, probably just as old as hers, that had been left untouched on the outside and was about one-third the size of Penny's. In spring her beautifully tended garden became a palette of colors that then changed with each season. Beyond the back lawn lay a marsh, the abode or hostel of great white and blue egrets, herons, whooping cranes, and smaller species I was unable to identify. A discreet wooden walkway led through the marsh to a half-moon sandy beach with a view of Shelter and Gardiners Islands. Penny lived in that paradisal setting—to be sure less paradisal in the winter— all year now, complaining that she could no longer afford an apartment in the city, but, I was convinced, secretly pleased to be a full-time gardener and bird-watcher. The reason for finding a pied-à-terre in New York out of reach was banal. Her husband was poorer when he died some ten years back than anyone had imagined; he left her the house and just enough money to reach the limit of the marital deduction, the trusts of which he was a beneficiary flipped to benefit exclusively their two daughters, Buddhists living in West

Coast ashrams. It was a mystery why he hadn't been more generous to Penny, who had been a model wife insofar as anyone knew and had nursed him through a stroke that left him paralyzed from the waist down until a second stroke finally killed him. We never discussed it. He wasn't someone I had ever liked.

I met Penny in the fall of my senior year, in September, judging by the sunny and warm afternoon I remember. She and her best friend, Francie, were selling subscriptions to something or other. They were very pretty. Penny brown haired, well made, with brown eyes and a turned-up nose, Francie taller, very blonde, and, I thought, probably too soft to touch, like uncooked dough. Whatever it was they were peddling, I subscribed. I couldn't think of any other way to justify lingering and engaging them in conversation. The ploy worked. I took Penny to see *High Noon* that evening at the University Theatre. It was the kind of film the UT showed over and over. I got to hold Penny's hand at the theater and to kiss her on the mouth when I dropped her off at the dorm after a hamburger at Cronin's. She lived at Moors, one of the Radcliffe Quadrangle dormitories. We'd had a good time, but I wasn't surprised when she kept her lips resolutely closed. In the weeks that followed we saw each other at least twice a week. We returned to the UT and laughed our heads off at *Kind Hearts and Coronets*, and to Cronin's where I was able to persuade the waitress, who was my pal, to serve Penny a beer; we necked in my car which I parked in the darkest spot I could find on Memorial Drive; I took her to dinner at the Henri IV. We made progress. She opened her mouth. She let me touch her breasts, at first only through her cardigan. A couple of dates later, she unhooked her bra and put her hand on my crotch. I got to push aside her undies. The classmate who had been my roommate since our freshman year got permission to take the year off and join a dig in Anatolia. Being suddenly alone, I was lucky enough to be assigned to a single suite in Eliot House, the fulfillment of the dreams of every sex-starved member of the house. The football season had begun. On Saturday, Harvard was playing some unimportant team, Dartmouth or Brown, at Soldiers Field. Penny didn't confess to any interest in the game and, more breathlessly I thought than usual, accepted my invitation to spend the afternoon studying in my living room. We might drop in on one of the after-the-game parties, I told her, or go directly to dinner at the Henri IV. I had made a reservation. And then, the day before, something happened to me that doesn't seem to happen to people these days; anyway, one doesn't hear about it.

I was winning 8–3 the fifth game of a squash match when I collapsed on the floor of the court with intolerable pain in my stomach. The guy I was playing against knelt down, felt my head, and asked if it was a cramp. I couldn't answer him.

I'm going to get someone, he told me.

We were playing at the Hemenway Gymnasium. I may

have passed out. I felt cold water on my head and shoulders in addition to the pain. When I opened my eyes, I saw one of the coaches.

Holy Christ, he was saying to the guy who'd gone to get him, you stay with Gardner. I'm going to call an ambulance.

It turned out to be a ruptured appendix, the consequence of the tummy ache I'd made it a point to ignore over several days, the infection so rampant in the stomach cavity that the surgeons decided it had to be cleared before the little stump itself could be removed. The operation took place at Mass General in Boston. I remained there for three weeks, then was taken to New York by ambulance for three weeks' rest at home. When I returned to Cambridge, the dean of students suggested that I might want to withdraw for the rest of the fall semester. I could return to the college in the spring, and then complete my degree requirements next fall. It had occurred to me that something of the sort was in the cards, and I had thought about it during the long weeks in my parents' apartment. I thanked the dean and told him I'd rather work very hard and not take advantage of the leave he offered. I'd done a good deal of reading in the city in order to keep up, and I thought I'd be all right. The reasons for making my life so hard? They ranged from one that was frivolous—I wanted to be sure I could keep my single suite—to another that was not. I had arranged to write my honors thesis under the supervision of a brilliant young government professor, Adam Ulam, with whom I had become friends largely due to his being a resident tutor at Eliot and a regular at the lunch table. I knew that he was scheduled to be away the following year, which meant I would have to find another thesis supervisor in the government department ready to take me on and would miss his hardheaded but sympathetic approach to my ideas.

A day or so after I returned to Cambridge, still feeling like hell, I called Penny. She wasn't at the dorm. She didn't call back. A couple of days later, I called again. She came to the telephone and sounded evasive. No, she couldn't meet me for tea at Hayes-Bickford; no, she couldn't meet me at Cronin's; she had so much work she had trouble keeping her head above the water. Could I call in a couple of days? I did. The girl on bells, the Radcliffe term for the student at the telephone switchboard, said they'd look for her. The search took awhile. It turned out she wasn't in, after all. There was a suppressed giggle in the voice of the girl on bells. All right. I could take a hint. Besides, I recalled that she hadn't come to see me at the hospital and hadn't called after I was transported home to the city. Shyness, I had thought, or some quirk of Philadelphia Main Line upbringing. I didn't give a whole lot of thought to this unexpected brush-off. I was working too hard, methodically making up for the time lost to my appendix. It wasn't easy, even though I was no longer on the squash team and the hours I'd spend on the court could now be given over to coursework. What's more, I felt better but not nearly recovered. And then I had a chat with Penny's friend Francie. She sat down next to me at the counter at Leavitt & Peirce where I was having tea and an English muffin between classes and, after commiserating about my long illness, asked whether I'd heard about Penny.

What about her? I replied.

She's going steady with McBride.

Is she? I grunted.

I doubt that I would have pursued the subject even if the name had been that of any one of the dozens of undergraduates I knew more or less vaguely and about whom I had no particular feelings. McBride was a man I loathed. The feeling, I believe, was instinctive: we had lived in the same entry of Wigglesworth in our freshman year, on the same floor, and there was something about his pale, self-satisfied blond face, his protruding eyes, and supercilious St. Paul's School party-boy manner that set me on edge. In the course of the year, my dislike only hardened and enveloped the roommate, who'd also gone to St. Paul's and, like McBride, was from Colorado. Copper-mines money, someone who'd been at school with them informed me.

My apparent lack of interest didn't discourage Francie.

They haven't gone all the way yet—she giggled—but they might as well.

She went on to describe, in such detail that I hoped no one at the counter was paying attention, Penny and McBride's activities, the principal goal of which, it seemed, was to bring him relief. But perhaps Francie didn't give McBride justice, and Penny was having a grand time too. I don't think I was a prude, and in my junior year a graduate student with thick eyeglasses and a pageboy haircut took my virginity. We got along well and probably would have still been together if she hadn't left for Europe on a Fulbright. Had it been anyone other than McBride, I might have laughed at Francie's story and said something like, Somebody's been showing them the ropes. I might have even tried to get Penny back, on the theory that there were riches there that should not be left unexplored. But the ignominy was too great. I told Francie I was going to be late for class, paid the check, and never gave Penny another call. In fact, I don't believe we saw each other again until a dinner in the city that Valerie and I attended after I returned to New York to take up my position as a senior editor of *Time*. We greeted each other with great enthusiasm, unfeigned on my part, discovering that we were still friends. I studied her husband with interest. He was a middle-aged but otherwise plausible version of McBride: Yale, instead of Harvard, manifestly nourished by a trust fund, a vice president of some commercial bank, and proud member of a racquet club the necktie of which he sported.

On the whole, I thought, not an unlikely Harvard-Radcliffe story, from the first boy-girl meeting in the Quadrangle, through being sweet and not so sweet on each other and a reunion at a fancy party in a Fifth Avenue duplex, to a low-key pleasant "won't you come to dinner" friendship in the Hamptons.

———

Penny's dinner turned out to be pretty much as I had expected, but I had a good time, seated between her and the lady painter. I was on Penny's left. On her right was the former ambassador who so occupied her that she never turned the conversation in my direction. That was all right with me. The lady painter had the New England looks I like, and she talked a blue streak, about her Bostonian relatives, some of whom I had known at school or at college, her failed prior marriage to a Jewish art history professor who had decidedly not fit in, her current husband who was a sweetie, and her art. I'd been to one of her shows, and the work was something I thought I could discuss. She must have thought so too, judging by her volubility, and invited me to her studio the following week. I accepted and resolved to buy a small view of Peconic Bay, of the sort I'd seen and liked. No sooner had the words that I was planning to be back in Bridgehampton the following weekend, and would be happy to stop by on a Sunday afternoon as she suggested left my mouth than the familiar dreary thought took over. What in the name of all of the gods on Olympus would I do with another painting? Even after Valerie's depredations I thought there were too many paintings and drawings on my walls, too many books on the shelves, too many kitchen utensils and too much china in the city and Bridgehampton kitchens, too much stuff that either Barbara and Rod would squabble over or, without so much as a good look, consign to the Salvation Army or big black trash bags. I should be selling off the stuff, or giving it away, not adding to it. The counterthought wasn't far behind: it doesn't matter, it won't be my problem, why not give this nice woman pleasure and prop her little landscape against the wall on my desk? An old friend's house, a quarter of a mile away, had been sold because he had suffered a light stroke that left him diminished. He no longer wanted to leave his apartment. The real-estate promoter who bought the house demolished it so fast, one thought it was done overnight. Now he was putting up in its place a structure twice as large and, it seemed to me, badly placed on the property. The house that was demolished was old, although not so venerable as mine, and very comfortable. The garden had been the site of Fourth of July and Labor Day parties to which every writer, editor, and literary agent in the Hamptons looked forward. It was a terrible slight not to be invited. Was this the fate reserved for my house as soon as the kids sold it? Barbara wouldn't be able to buy out Rod's share, it would come to way too much money, and I couldn't imagine her wanting to spend summers in Bridgehampton if she had to share the house with Rod and Carla. Putting it on the market would be the natural move.

Don't leave with everybody else, Penny whispered as coffee was served. We haven't seen each other in an age. Let's catch up!

I nodded and lingered on the bench before the open fire. Soon, she had finished goodbyes and sat down beside me.

Would you like a brandy or a single malt scotch? I've also got a very fancy Calvados.

I'd love one of each, I replied, but I can't. I had a bourbon before dinner and two glasses of your excellent wine.
If I have another drink, I'll never make it home. Not in one
piece.

She moved closer to me and said, You could sleep over! I
serve a very good breakfast.

Lead me not into temptation, I replied. This old man has
to take eight pills at bedtime and four when he gets up,
most nights he needs a sleeping pill—a mild sleeping pill,
but badly needed—and by eight-thirty he has to be at his
desk or wherever else he has put his computer and work on
his wretched book.

All right, she said, pouting, I'll give you a rain check. Next
time bring your pills and your laptop. No more excuses!
Anyway, I'm not going anywhere unless you ask me to drive
you home, so I'll have a drink.

Holy Moses, I said to myself. An octogenarian coquette!

She came back bearing a snifter with a good dose of brandy
or Calva in it. I'd moved into an armchair catty-corner to the
fireplace. She sat down again on the bench.

This is very good stuff, she said. Billy—that was her sinologist nephew—brought it to me when he came back from a
conference somewhere in Normandy. Caen, I think. Hugo,
don't you find it nice that we're friends after all these years?
You've probably forgotten, but I behaved badly. Took up
with that awful McBride while you were so sick!

I laughed. You discovered he wasn't Prince Charming!
Well, I wasn't either.

He was perfectly awful, but it took me months to figure it out. I was a real goose. But you forgave me?

Of course. At that age people break up all the time. Besides, I was in a sort of daze, catching up with coursework, getting my thesis done. I wasn't feeling any too well.

It could have been so different if I'd just been smarter!

Penny, that was more than sixty years ago! After graduation I went into the army. They shipped me off to Europe. You were still in college when I came back. I'd lost track of you. I don't know when you married Dwight. But by the time I was demobilized and came back to work in New York, we weren't the same people who met that afternoon during your freshman year. And there have been so many twists and turns since....

Dwight was her late husband.

How did the terrible Valerie get into the picture?

Valerie? She's not really terrible. She married a guy who was too old for her. Apparently, that didn't bother her for many years and then, finally, it did. And she was able to find a younger man, younger than she, I'm told, and handsome. Can you blame her if she decided that sticking it out with an old wreck isn't for her? It came as a shock, and made me desperately sad, but I've cooled off about it. We all should. How did she get into the picture? I was living in Paris, I'd just become the bureau chief there, I met her, and I thought she was great. That was just after I had made another big mistake. Not as big in retrospect as marrying Valerie, but still, even a hundred years later it's painful.

It was true that I was putting in long days working on my book. Miraculously, it was near completion. My editor liked what she saw and said, Step on it. We'll get it into production and out before the end of the year! Perfect timing! It will be a hit. I had my doubts. How would my taking down of George W. Bush compete with the slow-motion train wreck that I foresaw the election cycle would turn into?

But I wasn't going to argue. Jeb Bush's likely presence in the race and the book's serving as a review of Bush family obtuseness might do the trick. Work notwithstanding, if the weather was good, I went to Bridgehampton on weekends. I loved the house, and I'd always worked efficiently there. Penny seemed to be giving a dinner just about every Saturday and didn't fail to invite me. I was glad to accept after a day's work and solitude, unless I was dining at my cousin Sally's. I'd gotten fond of Penny and accustomed to the drive to Springs, but I'd known Sally as a little girl, and she had priority. She was the one remaining link to my past, and, last but not least, I looked forward to having my namesake Hugo jump in my lap and comment grumpily in French-bulldog-speak on current events and the canine condition. I was amused by the new assiduity of these two ladies, and the kaleidoscope of their female dinner guests. Penny had either given up on flirting with me or wasn't afraid of exposing me to competition. I asked Sally what she thought was going on.

She laughed and said, Don't you understand? You're an eligible bachelor! You're a catch.

It was my turn to laugh.

I'm quite serious, she continued. You have a nice house in the best part of Bridgehampton and an apartment on Carnegie Hill in the city, it's believed that you have just enough money, you seem to be in good health, anyway you get around without a walker or Canadian canes, you haven't lost your marbles, and you're not bad looking. You weren't ever an Adonis, but all things considered for your age... You have your own teeth, your own hair, and you're trim. On top of that, you have a reputation! As a big-time magazine editor and a writer. What more could a divorcée or widow living around here want in a guy to shack up with? And what more could a hostess like Penny—or me!—want in a male guest to grace her dinner?

Ask Valerie! I told her.

I finished my book soon after Jeb Bush, to no one's surprise, announced his candidacy. There would be work to do on the manuscript once the fact-checkers, copy editors, and legal reviewers got through, but for the moment I felt I was on vacation. I swam desultory laps in the swimming pool, walked on the beach, swam in the ocean if the surf wasn't too rough, read, and enjoyed my life as a newly minted eligible bachelor. Roddy, Carla, and their children spent the Fourth of July weekend with me in pleasant harmony. I had no news from Barbara. Not since our lunch at my club, a week or so after which she sent me an email that read: I guess I lost my cool, Barbara. The bound galleys of my book were sent out to publications and pundits superfast at the beginning of September. The vibes were good. Toward the end of September, I received an invitation to a conference in Paris on American politics, to be held at the École de sciences politiques in mid-October. My initial inclination was to say no. Then I thought about it for a week and said yes. Unexpected nostalgia was a factor in my decision, as was the prospect of debating issues with some of the other participants whom I had known for years. The determinative factor, however, was a telephone call I received from Dr. Klein, my combination urologist and oncologist. I had seen him ten days earlier as part of our watchful-waiting routine. The examination including the dreaded fingering of my anus showed that everything was normal. But now the results of the blood tests had come in and revealed that, as Dr. Klein put it, my PSA figures had gone through the roof.

I want you to have a biopsy right away, he told me.

All right, I replied, I have nothing against having a biopsy but not right now. I'm going abroad to participate in a conference and will be away for several weeks, so nothing can be done before I return, regardless of what the biopsy tells you. I'll check in as soon as I return.

There was a silence, and then he said, I really recommend that you have the biopsy and if necessary start treatment even if it means canceling your trip.

I understand and respect the advice, I told him, and I hope that you'll forgive me if for once I don't follow it. I'll check in as soon as I get back.

What was the poor man to do? He wished me good luck.

I didn't tell him that the news of my rebellious PSA had in fact filled me with a mixture of excitement and relief. If those cancer cells were spreading, perhaps had already spread, my end was foreseeable and manageable. Not for me Alzheimer's or a stroke leaving a twisted face or paralyzed limbs or the dreaded tremors and debility of Parkinson's. I'd be plenty able to take that one-way trip to Zurich, but first I'd put my affairs in shape for my departure. I wasn't thinking of money and bequests. My will was up to date; I wasn't going to change it to cut out Barbara or diminish what she'd receive because she was an idiot. It wasn't worth it and, anyway, I loved her. I meant my personal possessions, none of them really important. Furniture I had inherited, paintings of little value, books, doodads collected over a lifetime. I'd dispose of as much as I could correctly. I didn't want the stuff to be profaned.

A cadence we used to sing in heavy-weapons basic training at Fort Dix when Company C hit the road drifted into my mind. I altered the words slightly and sounded off: Heidi, Heidi, Heidi ho! Heidi, Heidi, Heidi hi! Cancer cells are on the go! Cancer cells are on the go! Count cadence, count cadence, count cadence, count!

V

THE HOTEL ON RUE DU FAUBOURG SAINT-HONORÉ where I normally stayed when *Time* picked up the tab had become so expensive that I doubt any U.S. magazine or newspaper still put up its personnel there, even senior journalists and editors. Multimillionaire TV and cable personalities? Perhaps. Wholly different rules might apply. It was certainly out of my reach unless Paris became, like Zurich, a Styx port of call and I checked into that onetime home away from home knowing that the next morning I'd take the last taxi ride of my life to a discreet clinic somewhere in Passy or Neuilly. In fact, my old hotel had changed too much for me to regret it. When I stopped by the bar there a few years back to have a drink with an old *Paris Match* colleague, I found most of the club chairs in the lobby occupied by overweight Levantine types busy on their cell phones, fat legs spread out as though to show off the owner's crotch, and other personages, no less obese or vulgar, whom my long experience of the Soviet Union taught me to recognize instantly as Russian businessmen. Presumably oligarchs, with business in Paris or on their way to the Côte d'Azur or back. Do other kinds of Russians exist? Of course, for instance, dissidents, whom Putin locks up or orders assassinated. It was all too bad. My hotel had been short on charm, but the location was terrific, the rooms comfortable, and, in the basement, there was a swimming pool. Above all, it had been so respectable! My dear aunt Hester, who left to me the house in Bridgehampton, and her ancient Hartford, Connecticut, lady cousins had been frequent guests. But the decadence of hotels was general. During the same visit to Paris I also had drinks at the bar of two or three of the other great Parisian palaces and found the clientele no more attractive, not even at the Ritz, which was about to close for a total makeover.

Needing another solution, and reluctant to rent one of the apartments offered to tourists where you end up keeping house when you would rather be doing other things, Valerie and I took to staying at a little hotel at the start of the rue de Bourgogne, recommended years ago by Paris *Vogue* colleagues whose office, before they were obliged to move to colorless avenue Hoche, was practically next door, on the place du Palais-Bourbon. That hotel had suited us perfectly, but when I telephoned to reserve my usual room I discovered that the hotel had changed hands and the charming manager who had become a friend had been let go, her place taken by someone who didn't recognize my name although I must have stayed there at least fifteen times. In fact, none of the personnel I'd known seemed to be still around. Since my cousin Sally went to Paris at least once a year, I asked her advice. She named a hotel in the *sixième*, on the rue Cassette, steps away from Saint-Germain-des-Prés and a five minutes' brisk walk from Sciences Po, where I would be spending most days.

It's very quiet and very charming, she said, you'll love it. Everybody there is so kind! It has a little garden where you can have a drink or even lunch if the weather is as warm as now.

As always, she was right. From the moment I walked in, I knew the place would suit me perfectly. My first evening, I walked over to the Lipp. It was a quarter of eight, a very busy time, and I thought I'd have a long wait before I got a table or would be sent upstairs, to the Siberia reserved for undesirables, to which I had never yet been consigned. To my great astonishment, Monsieur Gilles, the combination Cerberus and Saint Peter of that establishment, who decided, first, whether to admit you at all, and, second, at what table and when you would be seated, had not retired. He was right there at the passage from the café to the restaurant and recognized me before I had had a chance to open my mouth. He stepped forward, his arms open to embrace me, and cried, Monsieur Hugo! It's been quite a while. Two, three years? Will you be dining alone?

I told him that yes, I was alone, it was as much as four years, and I was happy to see him, so unchanged, so obviously in good health.

Just like you, just like you, monsieur.

And then, speaking to a waiter, he instructed him where to seat me. In a prized place, it turned out, on a banquette without vis-à-vis, near the window giving on the boulevard. I ordered my principal favorites, *hareng à l'huile* and grilled andouillette, and a half bottle of the house Bordeaux, and thought of all the times I had eaten the identical meal in this brasserie starting in the years of my military service, through too many assignments to count that took me to Paris when I was still a foreign correspondent, all the way to my years as Paris bureau chief. Meals taken alone, with colleagues, with Valerie, and before her with other girls not all of whose names I felt certain I remembered. In fact, only one of them had mattered. As Valerie's culinary interests and activities took wing, she decided that the Lipp was a waste of time, and led—I won't say dragged—me to one chapel or temple of nouvelle cuisine after another, to old-time bistros that had been miraculously modernized by energetic new owners often freshly arrived from some province not previously associated in my mind with the summits of gastronomy, and, for the purposes of comparison and not always constructive criticism, to the classical greats: Le Grand Véfour, Taillevent, Lucas Carton, Maxim's. All in decline now, Maxim's indeed no longer a restaurant. Véfour had been my favorite. For some reason, Valerie had not liked it. I resolved to book a table the first evening I had no obligation at Sciences Po. Even if the *queue de boeuf* and the sweetbreads were not as I remembered them, neither the charm of the Palais-Royal nor the astonishing beauty of the eighteenth-century interior of the restaurant, its mirrors, its gilded woodwork, would have changed. It couldn't have. The interior was surely a legally protected landmark. Jeanne, Valerie's immediate predecessor, had loved to go there. In the end, I had treated her shamefully, but before that, while we were together, I was never one to refuse to go to a good restaurant. Besides, at the time, meals there were nicely affordable for an American spending U.S. dollars. I hated to think how much dinner there would cost now, assuming I had that *queue de boeuf* or sweetbreads, preceded by some sort of shellfish and followed by crème brûlée. Plus a half bottle of wine and a *fine*. It didn't matter. Hadn't I decided that in my case parsimony was foolish? It was also Jeanne who really liked to eat, her taste in food and restaurants being closer to mine than Valerie's, who introduced me to the bistro on rue du Cherche-Midi owned and managed by a couple with whom I became friends. The husband cooked; the wife was at the cash register. A fine traditional arrangement. The couple retired ages ago, but the restaurant might still exist. It would be nice to investigate. The Moroccan couscous hole-in-the-wall, less than a block away, where we used to eat the best couscous *merguez* in the world, was also one of her finds.

Jeanne. It was natural enough that I thought about Valerie more than I would have liked, while Jeanne had all but disappeared. Even though we had been together, depending on how you counted, more than two years. Perhaps as many as four. *Does the imagination dwell the most / Upon a woman won or a woman lost?* I certainly managed to lose Valerie and now wished I could say, Good riddance! Would that day ever come? It didn't help that her name and bits of unsolicited information about her and Monsieur Leblanc's activities had a way of popping up in my children's communications. The one that should have put me in a state of rage but in fact made me laugh was an email I received from Barbara a few days before leaving for Paris. I had not heard from her all summer.

Dad, she wrote, Rod says you're off to Paris for some sort of meeting and will be gone several weeks. Mom needs to be in East Hampton for a big culinary competition among some of the top chefs. She's one of the judges. Any problem if she and Louis stay in the house? Will your housekeeper be there to open the house and help? Is it still Gloria?

Signed Barbara. None of this "love," or "I love you," or "I hope you're well" stuff. I examined this message carefully. It looked genuine. It was certainly sent from her Gmail account. If anyone had hacked it and had gone phishing, why would he or she send such a ridiculous message, one that, in any case, displayed such a good knowledge of Barbara? I called Rod. Yes, he was at the office, and of course he would look at Barbara's email if I sent it to him. He called back within a half hour.

That's something, he said. She really should have asked you on the phone.

Perhaps. I shrugged. Probably, she didn't trust herself or

me not to hang up. The real questions are (a) do I answer, (b) do I tell her she's out of her mind, or (c) do I say, No problem, so long as they use one of the guest rooms. I don't want them in my bed. I'm tempted not to answer.

It isn't worth it, Dad. Barbs is Barbs. It's Mom who should have her head examined, but that's another problem. Why don't you take the easy way out and tell her it's okay? If you don't feel up to it, I can deal with Barbara for you. Just tell me Gloria's telephone number so they can give her a heads-up and anything else you'd like me to mention.

You're a hell of a good lawyer, I said. Motion granted. I'll email you the telephone number and the password for the burglar alarm. Barbara and your mom should thank you, even if they don't bother to thank me!

The next day's session at Sciences Po made me feel that I hadn't been wrong to attend the conference. My talk about the dynamics of the presidential election, to the extent one could distill them already from the primary season, was clearly what the group was eager to hear. It was fol-lowed by a discussion *à bâtons rompus* of themes I had evoked: the powerful and pervasive influence of the evan-gelical Christian right and its ability to relitigate issues seemingly settled—availability of abortion, decriminaliza-tion of same-sex relations between consenting adults, legal-ity of same-sex marriage—the festering racist resentment of President Obama; xenophobia directed at Latinos, legal and illegal, rampant even in areas of the country where their presence is minimal; a strange and in some ways touching nostalgia of Rust Belt working-class white males for a version of American life that may have never existed except in *The Best Years of Our Lives* and that, in any case, very few of them would have experienced. You get the idea. A typical American family. Mom, Pop, two little boys, and a little girl, all flaxen haired. Their bicycles are in the driveway. They've just ridden home from the Little League game, because Pop is back from work and soon it will be dinnertime! Pop has a steady well-paying job at the factory making washing machines or, a few steps up the social scale, at the insurance company or the local savings bank. The mortgage on the one-family house the family lives in has been almost paid down; the shiny Chevy in the driveway is owned free and clear; next summer the family will take a trip to the Rockies, and the summer after that to Florida. And is life like that now? Who are you kidding, mister? With competition from countries where they pay one dollar per hour and plants here shutting down or moving to Mexico, it's time to Make American Great Again!

I attended the afternoon session on defense problems related to NATO's troop levels and combat readiness, and the special vulnerability of the Baltic republics. These were places I had visited in my Moscow bureau chief days when they were part of the Soviet Union. Melancholy backwaters, incomprehensible languages drowned in a sea of Russian, a population that seemed somewhere between unhappy and surly. I hadn't gone back since their independence and found I was wishing them well with real emotion. All the same, jet lag or just plain fatigue hit me hard by the time that panel ended, and I asked to be excused from the dinner to follow at Hôtel de Lutèce. Back at the hotel I lay down and fell into a sleep so profound that I had no idea where I was when I woke up or what time it might be. I looked at the alarm clock. In fact, I'd slept less than an hour. It was not too late for dinner. I decided I'd go to the restaurant on the rue du Cherche-Midi.

Unchanged. Same bistro furniture, bustle, lighting, chatter of diners busy with their meals. I hadn't made a reservation, but I could be seated. When I asked about my friends, the owners I once knew, I wasn't surprised to learn they were dead. They were a few years older than I, and their lives had been much harder than mine. Jean working tirelessly, from five in the morning, when he went to the Halles or Rungis to buy meat, vegetables, and fruit, until midnight or later, after he had drunk the last little *fine* with clients he had befriended who were still lingering at their table. Never mind that, in the meantime, he had been in the kitchen, standing in the heat of his stove and his ovens, his forearms like the forearms of most chefs, covered with burns. The menu hadn't changed either. I ordered leeks followed by sautéed foie gras, my favorite dish there, to which I had been introduced by Jeanne. Jeanne, the "woman won"—the woman I had banished from my life. I hadn't forgotten her; that was impossible. But I no longer knew anything about her. Years ago, when I first began to use a laptop, my secretary transferred addresses from my Rolodex, pocket calendars, and Lord knows what else to the contacts file on the laptop. From laptop to laptop, and then to my cell phones, this record of days and hours reduced to telephone numbers, street names and numbers, and later email addresses has accompanied me. As though on a bet, I opened my cell phone and typed Jeanne Brillard in contacts. Quai Anatole France came up, followed by a Solférino telephone number. That was about like finding that your old sweetheart's telephone number is Butterfield 8! Of course, I thought. This is not where she lived when we were together. Her little apartment was on the Right Bank, on the rue de Penthièvre, more or less behind the Bristol. Anatole France might be where she moved after she got married. Perhaps after some intermediate relocations. I would have copied the address and telephone number into whatever notebook I was using when I received a change-of-address notice. Would she have sent me one? Could it have been part of a wedding announcement? I didn't remember receiving one, but somehow I was pretty sure that she got married a few years after Valerie's and my marriage. The only member of Jeanne's New York set I still ran into occasionally might have told me. She and Jeanne had been close and saw each other in Paris.

Tarte Tatin was on the menu. That too was a dish Jeanne liked. I ordered it, adhering to the theory that it made absolutely no difference if I gained a few pounds. It was a smart move. The tart was every bit as good as I remembered.

One thing leads to another. Why not give Jeanne a ring and ask to see her, if only so that we can each take stock of the games time has played with us? I would put the concierge at the hotel to work on modernizing that Solférino number. I was taking part in a panel at Sciences Po the next morning, but unless I changed my mind I would call her after lunch.

VI

S HE ANSWERED THE PHONE herself. I'd recognize that
voice anywhere, I thought.

Hello, Jeanne! It's me. You won't believe it. Hugo.
Hugo Gardner. I'm in Paris for a conference. Yesterday evening, I had dinner at Chez Joséphine. I thought of you and
decided to call.

Hello, Hugo. That's very nice.

We were speaking French. When we first met in New York
at a party given by some young French people, the inter-
nationals, as she called them, we spoke French, and that
became our language, a habit neither of us tried to shake.
Her English was very good although it sometimes went a
tiny bit askew, and she had almost no accent. We'd switch
to English instantly when we were with English speakers.
I didn't correct her English, and even though I had asked
her to point out my mistakes she almost never did. That's
not true. She'd correct me when I said *le* instead of *la* or

vice versa, a trap that practically everyone for whom it's an acquired language falls into.

She had gone silent.

Faced with the choice between bidding her goodbye and trudging on and saying something, I ventured: It would be nice to catch up, after all that time. Would you like to have lunch with me, or a drink, or dinner? It would give me immense pleasure.

After what felt like a long moment, she said, But don't you think that catching up will be a big project? But yes, of course, she'll be glad to see me. Tea or a drink tomorrow at six? You have the address? We're a few steps away from the museum. Third floor. She went on to give me her building's code. If you get it wrong, please call. Someone will come down to let you in.

I went to the Musée d'Orsay the next afternoon and to my surprise found there was no line to get in. At a little after five, I walked along the quai to the place du Palais-Bourbon, had an espresso and a cognac, and bought what I thought was a beautiful and discreet small bouquet of roses at the florist's at the corner of the rue de Bourgogne. So armed, I doubled back to the corner of Anatole France and rue de Solférino. At six sharp I rang Jeanne's doorbell. A man dressed in black opened, took the flowers from my hand, and said, Madame la comtesse is in the library. Please follow me.

It was a large room with plenty of light, its windows looking out over the river and the Tuileries, dark mahogany
boiseries, books in leather bindings on the shelves, leather-
covered sofa and armchairs, and a large Empire desk. On
it a laptop and an Empire-style lamp. Not a scrap of paper,
no newspaper or periodical. She rose to greet me and held
out her hand. I didn't kiss it. The gesture would have struck
me as theatrical. It made me sad that she hadn't offered her
cheek.

You're old, Hugo, she said, but otherwise not much
changed. Still thin, still elegant, but so serious! Much more
serious than in the old days. Have you forgotten how to
laugh, *rigoler*?

That's entirely possible, I said trying hard to smile, I do
seem to laugh less and less. But I'm truly glad to see you.
That's already giving my mood a huge lift.

Her face was the same, I thought, almost unwrinkled,
a benefit of the tiny layer of fat that had always given her
features a doll-like roundness. She wore a black djellaba of
such refinement that I was sure she had found it at Saint
Laurent, place Saint-Sulpice, rather than at a Moroccan
souk. If she had gotten stouter, it didn't show. The beautiful
garment made her look regal.

The man in black returned with my roses now in a vase.
She exclaimed over them and asked what I would like to
drink. I yearned for a large bourbon, but this was a French
household. Traditional too, it seemed. I didn't think a bourbon was in the cards.

Scotch whiskey and soda, I said, a good deal of whiskey and not too much soda.

Madame la comtesse was going to have a glass of champagne.

Thus instructed, the man withdrew only to return with astonishing speed bearing our drinks. Meanwhile, Jeanne had motioned for me to sit on the sofa and sat down at the other end.

Tell me about you, she said. Are you married?

I was, until less than a year ago. Valerie, my wife, left me.

Valerie! That's the woman for whom you dumped me!

I nodded. I'm afraid that's true. She left, without any warning, for a younger man. Younger than she. A Frenchman. In fact, a *bistrotier*! Owns a couple of trendy restaurants in New York and possibly one somewhere in France. I'm a little vague about him. As you can imagine, we've never met.

All those Gardners and ... what's your mother's maiden name?

Choate.

All those Gardners and Choates must be turning over in their graves!

No doubt, and with reason.

And you have children, with Valerie, I assume.

Yes, a son who is a lawyer in New York, himself married, with two children, and a younger daughter married to a dermatologist in Wellesley. She also has two children but doesn't have an occupation unless being nasty to her father qualifies as a trade.

That's too bad. Daughters are supposed to be nice to their daddy. And you're retired from your magnificent job, and you've written an amusing book about Clinton. I've read it and laughed and laughed. You see, I keep up—more or less.

Yes, I'm retired, and yes, I wrote that book. Saying it made you laugh is the greatest compliment yet! And I've just finished one about George W. Bush and Dick Cheney. I don't know whether it will make you laugh or weep. And now it's my turn to ask you a question or two.

No, I get to put one more question first: Why have you such a sour expression?

It could be, I answered, laughing, because the face is the mirror of the soul, or it could be because I have an almost permanent ache in my lower back. Not to worry! No cutting and sewing seems required. Just some steroid shots every six months or so. It does give one a sort of grimace.

Her face expressed genuine sympathy and for a moment I thought she would slide over on the sofa and perhaps rub my shoulder, if not my lower back. But she restrained any such impulse as there was and said, I'm so sorry. You should try acupuncture.

Thanks, I replied. Done it. Nice fellow. I like the Chinese. Zero results. But this backache is such an old friend, I might miss it if it were gone! And now it's really my turn. You're married, I think. Still married?

Oh, yes, still married. Two years after you dumped me, I met Hubert de Viry and we were married a few months later.

Now, Jeanne! I behaved badly. It was a big mistake. But there's a statute of limitations. Please forgive me.

I think I have forgiven. But I can't forget. Bad behavior and cruelty are just that. You can't explain them away. But don't call what happened a mistake. How is one to know the end of a story that hasn't been written? Could you foresee the end of your story with Valerie? How can we tell how it would have been between you and me?

One can't. One can hope. One can try to stay the course.

Really, Hugo! What did "stay the course" mean to you then?

Fair point. I'm not sure. Have you and Hubert children?

She shook her head.

Hubert couldn't have children.

I'm sorry.

I didn't say anything more, but I recalled vividly how much she wanted children. In fact, her harping on it was one of the things about her that drove me up the wall. Not because I had some philosophical objection to having children—stuff about not bringing them into this cruel world—or because my misanthropy extended to infants and little boys and girls, but because the life I led, as an increasingly busy and committed foreign correspondent, seemed to me totally incompatible with raising a family. Considering how Barbara feels about my role in her life as a father, I can't help thinking I was right. What happened when Valerie took the place of Jeanne? First, by the time we got married I had become bureau chief in Paris and was no longer rushing off to the four corners of the globe. Second, Valerie, who only talked about children in a pleasantly general way, in a manner of speaking took matters into her own hands. She had been using the diaphragm and stopped putting it in. The natural result followed. When I gave voice to my astonishment at her missing her period and testing positive for pregnancy, she confessed with great real or feigned timidity and gave me the best blow job yet. There were others, equally good or even better, to follow as she refined her technique, but that lay in the future and at the moment I was so undone by pleasure that I couldn't stop thanking her for making me happy and bearing our child.

Jeanne must have read what was going through my mind—at least the part that concerned her.

I drove you nuts, she said, going on about wanting children. Look where it got me. Never mind! Would you like to meet Hubert?

Of course.

He is at home. Hugo, I have to tell you that he suffers from dementia. Advanced dementia. He doesn't speak. He babbles. It's aphasia, not paralysis. He can't remember words. Some of the time he knows who I am. Someone who is familiar, who's okay, I don't believe that the concept "wife" means anything to him. I'm probably like the male nurses who take care of him. Familiar and nice. He has remained sweet tempered. I'm told that's unusual. So far, he can swallow all right and doesn't have any physical symptoms other than general muscular weakness. I don't think he knows where he is, he can't find his way from one room to another, I think everything is a big gray blur. But that's probably a meaningless metaphor. The neurologists say it's not really Alzheimer's or frontotemporal dementia or some variation of Parkinson's but mixed dementia. Like all the horrors stirred into one cocktail.

How absolutely awful. Since when?

Since he was sixty-one or -two. More than fifteen years. That's when we first noticed something was wrong. He had to retire from the bank. Then things got worse pretty quickly. Would you like to see for yourself?

I nodded.

She pressed a button on the desk. When the man in black appeared, she said, We will call on Monsieur le comte in a few minutes.

Turning to me, she explained, That's so the nurse can tell him there will be a visit and make sure everything is in order.

It was another large room with windows facing the river. Walls covered with a brown tissue, many hunting scenes, two sofas, armchairs, and a very large wall television screen on mute showing a basketball game. On one of the sofas across from the TV sat Hubert. A large, stocky man, bald, with an aquiline nose. I was struck immediately by how carefully he was dressed: neatly pressed khaki trousers, polished loafers, rust-colored shirt opened at the neck with an ascot carefully tucked into it, dark brown V-necked cashmere pullover, cashmere socks matching the shirt. Jeanne told me later that there was no coffee table in the room because of the danger of his tripping over it.

Hubert, hello, hello, said Jeanne, speaking very loudly. This is a friend. Hugo. A very nice man. He has come to say hello! And over there is Victor, also a very nice man who helps Hubert.

She pointed to a man in a gray suit who got up from a chair near the window when we walked in.

How is Monsieur le comte this afternoon? Has he had his tea?

Yes, madame, he very much liked the cake.

Meanwhile Hubert, who had been looking from one side of the room to another, as though he were searching for Jeanne or for the friend who had come to see him, was smiling broadly and repeating, Hello, hello, hello...

Rather like a parrot, I thought.

In that case, said Jeanne, I think he could have his evening cocktail.

She sat down on the other sofa and asked whether I would like another whiskey.

A small one, I told her. Neat.

Good. I'll have a champagne. Victor, will you please tell Georges?

The man in black appeared. On his tray were Jeanne's drink and mine and a glass of a green liquid.

I raised my eyebrows.

It's Hubert's Suze. Jeanne laughed. His Suze! Victor, please offer Monsieur le comte his Suze.

Monsieur le comte, intoned Victor, advancing toward Hubert, if you please, your evening Suze. Very delicious! Just as always!

Hubert stopped saying hello and instead took up Suze! Suze! Suze! Victor held it for him carefully while the poor man sipped, actually sipped, the stuff.

It's so good! said Victor.

Good! Good! Good!

Suze is an awful aperitif the family of Hubert's mother made, and it made their large fortune, Jeanne said. Don't you know about Suze? It was wildly popular until not so long ago, and I believe people still drink it. It's supposed to have wonderful medicinal properties. Of course, the family sold the business. Soon after the war, I think.

We said goodbye to Hubert and Victor. Jeanne accompanied me to the foyer, and I understood that she expected me to leave.

Hubert is so wonderfully well taken care of, I said.

She nodded. We do our best.

It shows.

And then, not quite knowing how to put the question less incongruously out of keeping with what I had just witnessed, I asked, When can I see you again? Dinner? Name a day.

Do you think it's *utile*? Does it make sense?

I would really like it.

Many evenings his sister or nephew or nieces drop in. I

like to be at home when they come. Will you still be here next Monday?

I nodded.

Then Monday. Eight-thirty. Where shall I meet you?

I'm not sure I expected her to say yes, and I was momentarily nonplussed. Lipp? Relais Plaza? I ventured. Some other place you like? You used to like the Relais.

No, no. Let's go back to Joséphine.

I walked and walked and walked afterward, first toward the Invalides, where I lingered admiring the most beautiful veterans' hospital ever imagined and built, then across the Seine to the Right Bank where I followed the Cours-la-Reine to the place de la Concorde. There, overwhelmed by a strange happiness compounded of the whirlpool of feelings, some contradictory, awakened by seeing Jeanne and the beauty of the magnificent space that stretches from the two Gabriel buildings at the northern edge of the square all the way to the Palais-Bourbon, I doubled back to the Invalides and then beyond, to an address I remembered on the boulevard des Invalides, where a young Frenchman, Jacques Legrand, whom I met when I was serving with SHAPE in Fontainebleau, once had an apartment. Jacques became a friend and soon my best friend in France. At the time, after five years of boys' boarding school and four years at Harvard College with its parietal rules that allowed you to have women in your room from four to six on weekdays and from one to seven or perhaps eight on weekends, provided, of course, that you kept your door open, the freedom Jacques enjoyed at his pad, and the amorous passages at arms of which it was the scene, highlights of which he liked to relate, made my head spin. One of these, involving a great big girl of the strongly meridional type and an accent to prove her origins, who was not, Jacques claimed, his girlfriend, just a *copine*, a pal, living at the apartment for lack of another place to stay, particularly inflamed my imagination. It had to do with towel fights they had, before going to bed, or first thing in the morning, or while they dressed to go out, chasing around and slapping each other's naked buttocks. I don't think Jacques told me whether they made love before or after these fights or indeed whether they were even sleeping together. I was more than able to supply the missing data, with variations to suit my mood and my needs. It wasn't long before, strongly encouraged by Jacques, I was myself sleeping with this girl, at Jacques's place if he was away, or in a cheap but clean little hotel, of all places on the rue du Cherche-Midi, a few steps from the boulevard du Montparnasse and across the street from Joséphine, which did not yet exist, not anyway under the ownership I was to know so well. It was an experience like none other I've had, she was so large and strong, like a young mare. I thought she might break me. It didn't come to that because soon afterward I was demobilized and returned to New York. When I was in

Paris next, I didn't attempt to look her up. Jacques told me much later that she had an *atelier de mode* in Arles.

What if I rang Jacques's doorbell? Of course, the idea was absurd. He moved away already in the seventies, when he got married, and now lived off the rue de la Pompe, on the other end of town. There had been no answer when I called before I left Bridgehampton or the couple of times I tried his number since I arrived. I didn't know what to make of that, since he would have surely let me know if there had been a change of address. He and Lucie could be traveling, of course, or they could be at their new country house somewhere in Normandy, to which I had never been. I didn't have his telephone number there. Even a Luddite like he probably had a cell phone, but he had never given me that number. There had to be a way to find him. Damn the French! Minitel, their super-clever little computer, used to let you find anyone anywhere in France and do just about everything else for you short of buttering your baguette. Why did they shut it down? Possibly something else was available online, the equivalent of the white pages. I'd look into it after the morning session at Sciences Po. I'd also try the national telephone information service, if it still existed.

My spirits sank. This sort of thing didn't happen to me before I retired, when I had a full-time secretary who kept track of friends' comings and goings and their coordinates. I was tired and hungry. What about the Lipp? That required another long walk. I looked up and down the boulevard, hoping to hail a taxi. As usual, there weren't any cruising or waiting at the two taxi stands I passed. Call Uber? To what pickup point? The corner café was closed. I shrugged and marched on. Monsieur Gilles didn't fail me. He greeted me again like a long-lost friend and assured me that a table would be ready for Monsieur Gardner in five little minutes.

I wanted a drink before my meal and ordinarily would have asked for a bourbon, but some sort of automatism changed the words before they left my mouth. I ordered instead a scotch and soda. Though I surely didn't rub the bottle when the waiter set it on the table along with the little bucket of ice cubes and the siphon, my past with Jeanne rose like the genie from wherever it was stored, so fresh and present that tears ran down my cheeks. Automatism also took charge of my dinner: *hareng Bismarck, brandade de morue,* and a half bottle of Côtes du Rhône. Côtes du Rhône rather than the house Bordeaux? Certainly. The waiter is always right. It made no difference.

The story begins in New York, in 1977, at a Council on Foreign Relations meeting for Cy Vance, to which someone brought as a guest a *Paris Match* colleague, a correspondent dividing his time between the city and D.C. He greeted me joyously. I accepted his invitation to a party given the next evening by some young French people.

You'll see some pretty girls, he assured me.

It was as he said. Girls in little black dresses, immaculate white stockings, stiletto heels, strings of pearls, blond or very black hair immaculately coiffed, all slim, not a few

of them flat-chested, girls in their twenties or early thir-
ties. Also boys, except that I suppose one would say men,
less uniformly slender, imprisoned in tight-fitting double-
breasted navy-blue blazers with brass buttons, hair often
curly, grown out over their ears and shirt collars, tasseled
black loafers that could be improved by being polished,
knit navy-blue neckties. Commercial and investment bankers and associates in management consulting firms, the
initials HEC branded on their foreheads. École des hautes
études commerciales, reputed to be the best French business
school, admission requiring success in a competitive examination, an institution prized by a certain kind of French
bourgeoisie, but one I looked down on, as indeed I looked
down on diplomas from the Harvard Business School and
the like. Accounting I have always acknowledged as an
essential skill. But marketing? Case studies comparing wid-
get companies that succeed with those that fail? Management philosophy? By what sleight of hand had subjects that
belonged if anywhere in a souk or bazaar, where they might
be handed down from father to son or uncle to nephew,
been converted into an academic discipline taught at fancy
buildings on the Charles River by Distinguished Professors
of entrepreneurship, teamwork, developing mind-sets for
creative problem-solving, and on and on? A con game equal
to or perhaps surpassing the con game that twenty-five
years later George W. and Dick Cheney would be pulling on
the nation. Moving from group to group, eavesdropping on
conversations, I determined that there wasn't a physician,

veterinarian, or journalist except my *Paris Match* friend among them. One roly-poly man seemed to be an art dealer and another, who might have been his twin, an antiques dealer. This gathering took place in a new high-rise in the East Fifties, with a superb view of the Pepsi-Cola sign on the river out the living room window. I shook my friend's hand confidentially and affectionately, felt no obligation to take leave of the host whom I hadn't met, and prepared my exit, when my path was blocked by a particularly blonde young woman with particularly pretty regular features, a low-cut little black dress that struck me as being of *le dernier chic*, and three strands of pearls on her milk-white skin.

You're Hugo, Hugo Gardner, she asserted. Roland—that was my friend—told me you'd be here and pointed you out.

Her English was very pretty, just like she.

I agreed that such was my name.

Ah, then we can speak French. That's so much easier!

She rattled off essential facts: she was French, Parisian, had a diploma from Sciences Po and a *licence* (a sort of bachelor's degree) in law from the Sorbonne but no intention of ever practicing law, and she was in New York on an assignment of indeterminate duration doing public relations and research for Saint Laurent into expanding further in the ready-to-wear market. She'd so wanted to be a journalist, but so far it hadn't worked out. The openings for women except in fashion were close to zero, and she didn't want to write about fashion. She had hoped to do general reporting, not necessarily political, but society.... Could we talk about the profession—generally, of course—she wasn't going to ask for help getting a job!

I told her that nothing could give me greater pleasure, but I was on my way out, leaving the party. Perhaps another time.

Have you had dinner? No, obviously not! Have you a dinner date?

I shook my head. The answer to both questions was no.

Could we have dinner together? Do you like Turkish food? The answer was yes.

Then let's go to my favorite Turkish restaurant, on Second Avenue and Sixty-Eighth Street, near to where I live? It's excellent.

The food was very good. Even more remarkable was how she pressed her knee against mine, her smile leaving no room for doubt that it was what she intended. And she talked nonstop. The subject of journalism did not come up, but she told me that she had a younger brother, that her father had started out as an automobile-parts distributor—I sensed that she was gauging my body language, what did I think of that line of business?—and having done very well went into real estate. At first rental buildings, principally in the seventeenth, fifteenth, and fourteenth arrondissements. At present, he was also developing properties in Neuilly and near the Porte de Versailles.

That sounds fascinating, I said, and very remunerative!

Yes, she said seriously, very much so. He'd like me to go into the business with him, since I have my law degree and all that and, in his opinion, a good head on my shoulders, but I don't want to. Not while he's so vigorous and doesn't need family help. And he's got my brother. Not that he has very much of a head for anything!

Then she asked how much time I spent in New York.

Hard to tell, I explained, it depends on assignments. Perhaps one-third of my time? Perhaps less. But I have this small apartment here and consider the city my home port.

We'd finished our bottle of red wine, like me, she thought it generally went well with Turkish food, and the baklava dessert. The waiter brought our Turkish coffee and, bizarrely, fortune cookies. Customers like them, he explained. Mine said, Smile and the hurt will go away.

And yours?

She smiled: You will find out.

I asked for the check.

Hugo, she said, wouldn't you like to come up for a drink? I'm just around the corner.

We tore each other's clothes off as soon as her apartment door closed behind us. She had a mouth of infinite depth, small and perfect breasts, and when I put my hand on her labia I found they were streaming liquid. Her bedroom opened on the living room. I picked her up and carried her to the bed, but before entering her I exacted—no, they were willingly given—services that should have come after long intimacy. When I did enter, she shrieked. I found she had the gift of immediate and repeated orgasms.

I staggered home at four or five in the morning. There was an editorial meeting starting at seven-thirty and I needed to shave, bathe, and change my clothes. The meeting ended shortly after ten, and I called her. To my immense relief, she answered.

Jeanne, I don't know how to beg your pardon, I made love to you like a drunken thug. I've never done such a thing before. Please forgive me. I'll understand perfectly if you never want to see me again.

Tu es fou, you're nuts, she answered. I want to be with you, I want you inside me every night. All the time.

VII

WHAT WENT WRONG?

The sex continued. It became our principal occupation. She spent every night at my apartment, arriving after her work—she had an office somewhere at Saint Laurent—with a tiny carryall she called her *baise-en-ville*, fuck away from home, took a bath whether I'd already come home or not, and if I hadn't arrived yet waited for me in bed. At some point in the day, she found time to stop by her apartment and restock the carryall. She found new ways to offer herself, some of which were outside of my repertoire. I asked her where and how and from whom she had learned them. From books, she said, from books. During the orgasms she'd tell me that I was the best lover she had ever had, that there was no one like me. The hyperbole made me oddly uncomfortable. I was a young man in excellent health and physical condition. Erections came quickly. After the first excitement and the first ejaculation, my staying power became good and served me well in subsequent engagements, but no girl I had slept with before had expressed such enthusiasm, including several who knew me long enough to be in a position to compare.

Naturally, we didn't cook our dinners. We went out, to Gino's, one of my favorites, an Italian restaurant that no longer exists, to the Veau d'Or which has survived, to Jeanne's Turkish restaurant, and only rarely to Elaine's. I discovered that I wasn't eager to introduce her widely to my friends. The reasons were obscure then and they are even now. I certainly wasn't ashamed of her—why would I have been? She was so pretty and so strikingly well dressed and so very polite. Her making it obvious, in my opinion needlessly, that she was my steady girlfriend, that she was as much as living with me, surely was a factor. I liked to keep my private life private, and I liked improvisation. Thus, I was not pleased one afternoon when, having come home before she arrived, I found in the bathroom linen closet, tucked in under a stack of hand towels, her diaphragm and lubricants. It was too much domesticity and possession taking. The presence of her toothbrushes, toothpaste, and hairbrush above the washbasin was enough.

As I said, she was very well dressed, but the effects were sometimes disconcerting. I took her to the opera one Monday, to see *L'Elisir d'amore*, which to my surprise she had never seen in Paris. It had slipped my mind that Mondays, including that particular Monday, were since time immemorial part of my parents' subscription. Had I thought of it, I would have chosen another evening. Jeanne had been asking to meet my parents, but I was reluctant to introduce her. What would I have told Mother when she telephoned to ask a pointed question or two about this very charming young woman? But the fat was in the fire; there in the Grand Tier Restaurant, were my parents, at a table near ours, and there was no possible escape. It was a time when not wearing a bra was still a big deal for young women; Jeanne didn't need or wear one, and I heartily approved. I loved the constant availability of her breasts. It was also a time of the see-through top. Jeanne was wearing a white one, with her beautiful black silk Saint Laurent trousers, and to my horror I remembered that she had put a little lipstick on her nipples. She looked stunning, and my parents put on a good show of seeing only her face. We chatted amiably. I'm not sure that Jeanne noticed the strange paralysis that seemed to have afflicted them. Whenever the subject of meeting them again came up, I'd find an excuse posthaste. I didn't want Mother to ask, Do you mean that nice bare-chested young woman? And I didn't want to explain that my exquisitely polite parents were barricaded behind a stockade of unwritten rules and prejudice.

Jeanne had not yet begun to tell me about wanting to bear my children. That was to come later, but there was no restraining her desire to become part of the fabric of my life. Meeting my parents and my friends, accompanying me the two or three times I went away for the weekend during the months I spent in New York, were objectives of which I was continually and uncomfortably aware. In fact, I would have gladly taken her with me to Bridgehampton, but I was visiting my aunt Hester and her husband, and had I asked for permission to bring Jeanne they would have immediately wanted to know the nature of our relationship, and whatever I said would have been reported to Mother and start ricocheting in a manner I particularly wanted to avoid. My other expedition was to my parents' weekend place in Syosset, on the North Shore of Long Island. There could not be any question of my taking her there. Perhaps, given more time in the city, we would have arrived at a modus operandi that satisfied me. That she was willing to put up with what she occasionally called my manias, was amply apparent. And perhaps we would have broken up. The problem was solved by my unexpected promotion. It turned out that I had been brought back to the city in order to be given a second look by the managing editor. I passed inspection, was named Paris bureau chief, and within ten days moved to Paris. Jeanne said, Take me with you just for a long weekend. The memory will console me while we're separated. Of course, I agreed.

I was astonished by the promotion and immeasurably happy and proud. Paris! The city I had come to love as a schoolboy on vacations with my parents and to know very well during my army tour. And I was there as the bureau chief of the best news magazine in the world, the youngest bureau chief in the magazine's history. I don't think my head was swollen any more than it had always been. But I was consumed by passion for my work and determination to succeed beyond my bosses' and anyone else's expectations. The few hours each week I didn't spend at the office, attending press conferences at the Élysée, interviewing politicians, or playing squash on the rue Lauriston courts, I devoted to making habitable the little apartment I had rented on rue Marbeuf, within easy walking distance of the office. It isn't an exaggeration to say that I did not miss Jeanne at all, and it wasn't because I had found a substitute for the sex with her. Far from it, I had not gone out—in the old-fashioned sense of that expression, meaning that since I arrived in Paris I had not taken any girl out to the movies, a drink, or dinner. There were a couple of attractive women working at the *Time* office. I'm not sure what the company policy was, if indeed any sort of policy was in effect, but I disapproved totally of anything resembling an office romance, a disapproval that as I recall extended to *Newsweek* colleagues, on the theory that they were our direct competitors. No, I didn't miss Jeanne because I wasn't thinking about her. I hadn't forgotten that she was there thinking about me, indeed staying in touch. Naturally, just as I promised before leaving, I gave her my office telephone number and, when finally, after pulling many strings, I managed to have a telephone installed in my apartment, my home telephone number as well. She called frequently, her ability to reach me limited only by my work schedule and the time zone difference between New York and Paris, and we had long talks on

Sundays. She knew better than to call me before nine in the morning my time, three in the afternoon hers, that being the one day in the week when I didn't need to bound out of bed at six to speak to my supervisory contacts in New York, but at nine sharp the phone on my night table would ring, and I would hear her voice. It was in the course of one of those interminable calls, which had me guessing willy-nilly at the size of the phone bill she was running up, that she told me triumphantly that she had managed it: Saint Laurent had offered her a position in its press department in Paris. A wave of immense pleasure swept over me. I found I wanted her with a force and urgency I would not have thought possible. Soon, she had her little apartment on the rue de Penthièvre. We were still within walking distance of each other and resumed our New York routine with what seemed to me an even-greater intensity in our lovemaking. We had a new repertory of restaurants, Lipp and Joséphine and Relais Plaza, to which we added Fouquet's, and Taillevent for great occasions, and for very late meals Bar des Théâtres, on avenue Montaigne, across the street from the Relais. But Jeanne was a specialist at finding hole-in-the-wall bistros in the *premier,* the *huitième,* and in the neighborhood behind Notre-Dame de Lorette that had not yet become fashionable.

She didn't remain long in the press department of Saint Laurent. One evening, perhaps five months after her return to Paris, she invited me to dinner at Fouquet's and asked me to meet her there as soon as I got out of the office. I was to call her at my apartment to let her know that I was about to leave. This was a surprise because our habit was to meet at the apartment, fall into bed, and go out to dinner after a bath we would share in my surprisingly large bathtub. She was waiting for me and had ordered a bottle of champagne, which the waiter served as soon as I sat down.

What's the occasion? I asked. You should do this more often.

Perhaps I will. Guess what happened!

You've placed a fib in *Le Figaro* that Saint Laurent is making Anne-Aymone Giscard's fall wardrobe!

You're not even close! I've been offered a job doing book reviews at *Elle*, and I've accepted. Put that in your pipe and smoke it!

I was delighted and wildly impressed, and I told her so with all the eloquence I could muster. She had pulled off a truly amazing coup.

She took my hand, kissed it, and said, Hugo, I want you to do something for me, for us. Please come to lunch on Sunday with my parents. At their place in the country. It's right outside Melun. And don't make that face! I know you're free, you were planning to take me to Vaux-le-Vicomte.

That was perfectly true. I wasn't going to spoil her evening of triumph by saying something on the order of "I don't do parents." Instead, I told her that I'd be delighted. I'd never met her parents, and I'd never been to Melun. Two birds with one stone!

Three, she said, because afterward we can go for a long walk in the Fontainebleau forest.

The parents' house, an ugly sizable three-story late-nineteenth-century affair, stood in a truly handsome garden; really you could call it a small park. It had been planted and maintained with great care.

It's a horrible-looking place, Jeanne had warned me, but very comfortable. After Father bought it he installed really good bathrooms, a modern kitchen, central heating. And there's plenty of hot water, no matter how many people are taking baths.

She issued another warning. Mother is very religious. Very active in the local parish even though they're only there on weekends. Every Sunday there's a priest at lunch. Sometimes two or three. Of course, her whole family is from there.

I'll fit right in. I laughed. My great-great-grandfather was the Episcopal bishop of Maine, and my great-great-uncle Phillips Brooks was the Episcopal bishop of Massachusetts! I have clerical blood in my veins.

These guys are different, she replied very seriously.

They were. Three jolly fathers straight out of Daumier, barely contained by their soutanes, napkins tucked into their Roman collars, digging into the leg of lamb, flageolets, and potatoes dauphinoise. Whatever verses of the Gospel they had read, whatever sermon they had preached, they'd left them behind in the pulpit. Two years remained until the French presidential election, but their attention was fixed on the probable—the fattest padre thought certain—challenge Jacques Chirac would mount against Valéry Giscard d'Estaing. Jeanne's mother thought that was the height of ingratitude. Hadn't Chirac been Giscard's prime minister? She was shouted down, Jeanne's father joining the priests. Giscard was turning leftist, think only of his dealings with the Soviets, while France and the church needed at the helm a man of the right with strong principles and a will of iron. Chirac would have their prayers. I was grateful for this unexpected view of the discord dividing French society. Its depth, and especially the role of the church, were issues to which I had better give more attention. But to the possible detriment of my study of French politics, the subject that was then absorbing me, although it lay outside the field of my responsibilities, was the storm that had been gathering force in Iran ever since the toppling some months earlier of Reza Pahlavi, the shah of Iran. I was secretly searching for the case I could make to my bosses in New York that my background qualified me uniquely to report on it, even if the need to be in Tehran or Istanbul or Ankara might require me to take temporary leave from Paris. Meanwhile, the discussion of Giscard and Chirac continued and turned to their personal lives. Giscard is a *chaud lapin*, a horny lecher, volunteered Jeanne's father. The mother chimed in: One can't understand how Anne-Aymone puts up with it.

One of the fathers opined that this sort of behavior scandalized the flock and reflected badly on the president's office. The subject proved to be vast, but the conversation did move on, to his former prime minister. If you talk of horny, so is Chirac, so is Chirac! cried a padre. Father Grosmonde of Saint Thomas d'Aquin, in whose parish it is, tells me that Chirac walks his dog up and down the rue du Bac and on the quai only to pick up girls! A dog is great girl bait. But he and the dog have to come home! Bernadette—that was Madame Chirac—keeps Jacques on a short leash. This bon mot provoked an outburst of general merriment, but I was tuning out. These people were unbearably boring. The lunch was dragging on. Brie de Meaux—Jeanne's father knew the producer, he bought the cheese directly from him. We compared it with the Brie de Melun, in fact made by the mother's cousin. The Melun brie won, forks down. I wondered how I would make it through the dessert.

I had not really known what to expect from Jeanne's mother, father, and brother, and had given up trying to imagine their appearance. A man who had made his money distributing auto parts? And in small-time real estate, working his way up to wealth, the apartment on avenue de Wagram that I hadn't seen and had no desire to visit, and a country house somewhere near Melun? Would the father preside at table in a black Sunday suit? Complete with a double-breasted suit jacket? Or would he shed his jacket and sit at table in shirtsleeves, trousers held up by cheap black braces? Would the mother look like the stereotype of the lady behind the cash register in a black taffeta dress, her shiny black hair combed back into a tight bun? Gardners and Choates were hard at work on their snotty scion. But, so far as their apparel was concerned, the father and the mother would not have been out of place at a family lunch in Syosset! The father in dark brown corduroy trousers, an English-looking checkered shirt peeking out from under a crew-collar red sweater, elegant walking boots. The mother sported a plaid skirt, a green cardigan, and brogues. The kid brother was in blue jeans. And they were all three blond! How could it be otherwise? Where else would Jeanne have gotten her coloring?

I did make it through lunch, leaving, I believe, a good impression—*l'Amerloque*, the Yankee, speaks such good French, etc., etc., Jeanne seems so happy—but that visit, or perhaps Jeanne's change of job, marked a change in our relationship. Until then, we had principally talked, in no special order, about clothes, dishes we especially liked at restaurants we favored or intended to go to, films she wanted to see, and her desire to enter more deeply into my life. We didn't talk much about politics; in fact, hardly ever. I think she believed that since it was at the center of my work I preferred to leave discussion of politics at the office. The relative boredom of Jimmy Carter's third year in office may have also played a part. She thought that carrying his own garment bag and being seen on TV in a cardigan were not presidential. Unimaginable in French life. Now for the first time she was deeply involved with her colleagues, young journalists her age or a year or two older, lively and attractive, and here is where trouble began, she wanted me to become part of their *bande,* gang. As a senior and highly experienced reporter and now bureau chief, working for a publication like *Time,* I had so much to contribute! The problem was that however charming and bright and in the case of some of the women good looking I found her colleagues, they didn't interest me. After a quarter of an hour, their chatter began to irritate me. I wasn't amused by the parties they organized on the spur of the moment in one or another's apartment, with *gros rouge,* scotch whiskey because some of the men liked hard liquor, baguettes, dry sausage, *pâté de campagne,* and the eternal Brie. The books Jeanne was reviewing—she wrote little squibs—were almost all what is now called chick lit. She didn't really expect me to read them, but she'd tell me the plot, the character development, the setting, and wanted to know what I thought of the squibs. I'd do my best by questioning her, trying to test her conclusion, sometimes I tightened her text, but none of that was satisfactory to me.

My attention was riveted on Iran. I had been able to finagle a special assignment to Tehran in the summer and was able to report on the overwhelming violence of anti-American feelings, which had not been allayed by the Carter administration's decision to continue military aid and other gestures intended to atone for the president's faux pas in his New Year's toast to the shah in which he claimed that the shah was beloved of his people, and on the exodus from

Iran by all means, legal and illegal, of the Iranian upper class and whoever else could manage it. The U.S. embassy was under siege, though not yet occupied. The shah fled to Egypt. Some of this I witnessed in Tehran itself. I did background work in Ankara and Istanbul. Then, in October, Henry Kissinger, who has a prominent place in my gallery of charlatans and knaves, joined hands with David Rockefeller, then the chairman of the Council on Foreign Relations. Led by the nose by his friend Henry, David twisted the arm of the State Department and pushed aside whoever else in the Carter administration was firmly opposed to the move and arranged for the colossal mistake of having the shah admitted to the United States for treatment of his lymphoma. In November, Islamist students seized the U.S. embassy, and four hundred forty-four days of captivity began for the embassy personnel and the marines stationed there. I foresaw that resulting change in the geopolitical map of the Middle East and some of its short-term and long-term consequences. But it was time to stick to my Paris job and the presidential election that gave France its first Socialist president after some forty years of right-wing rule.

As I've just said, my mind was occupied. The bureau was functioning to my and New York's satisfaction. What was going wrong? To put it crudely, Jeanne's friends, whose number seemed to grow, irritated and bored me, and I could find no way to separate her from her *bande* except at night, when we were at last in bed and she offered herself with undiminished enthusiasm and inventiveness. But even there, all was not well. I noticed it, and I didn't think it was possible that she didn't. I no longer took her lovingly. I don't mean the thuggish behavior of which I had accused myself from the start. I knew that she liked it. She wouldn't have wanted it to change. I mean something subtler and far more unpleasant. Whether I was inside her or in her mouth, I was not seeking to give her pleasure or even to take pleasure in the act myself. I was attacking her. I was ashamed, ashamed to look her in the face at breakfast. Two weeks before the U.S. embassy in Tehran was overrun, I thought I found a peace offering. I took Jeanne to Madrid for the weekend. She had never been and embraced and covered me with kisses when I told her we were going. We stayed at the Ritz, learned the Ritz recipes for sangria and gazpacho, and, except for lunch breaks, spent daytime hours at the Prado. But my attacks on Jeanne's body only grew more violent. I don't mean to suggest that I ever hit her or became guilty of whatever other physical torments figure in the manual of bourgeois sadomasochism. It was entirely in the usual gestures; in the way each of those gestures maltreated her body. As we were heading for the airport, she said to me, You no longer make love to me, Hugo. You find ways to show that you wish I weren't there.

By then Valerie, the "woman lost," had already come on the scene. Innocently, to be sure, but she was there. My principal competitor in Paris and old friend, the bureau chief of *Newsweek*, said there was a sweet and very bright girl trying to get a foothold in Paris and finding it impossibly hard. She'd had a job in London and lost it. Really wanted to be in Paris. Crazy about French culture and the French. Would I have lunch with the two of them and see what could be done? She was indeed sweet and bright, a couple of years, I guessed, younger than Jeanne, and really strikingly pretty in the Audrey Hepburn style that someone of my generation couldn't fail to go for. Never mind. To be helpful to my friend and out of the goodness of my heart—so I told myself—I called in some chips at the *Herald Tribune* in Paris and New York and eased her way into a culture job, low level but still a culture job at a great newspaper that was the indispensable companion of Americans traveling or settled abroad, and started her on the path to her present TV culinary-expert glory. She was, as I said, very bright. The importance of what I had done wasn't lost on her. She invited me to dinner. I told her that was awkward, and I'd rather have a drink. Cinq Roo Daunou, said the darling child, thinking that the idea of Harry's Bar with its aura of American writers in the Roaring Twenties drinking themselves to death would appeal to me. I nodded pleasantly, we drank martinis, and I saw her home to a bourgeois building on a nearby street where she rented a maid's room. At the door, she offered me her lips, and after we'd embraced, keeping our mouths chastely closed, she said she hoped to see me again.

She did. I couldn't resist, I didn't really want to resist what I can only identify as American sex appeal. Pretty soon I explained that evenings were not a time when we could meet, that lunch was much better, and lunches became quick sandwiches at a café followed in the maid's room she rented by necking sessions the length and intensity of which reminded me of afternoons at Eliot House until, at last, she consented to go all the way. When she did, it was in some respects the opposite of Jeanne's giving herself. With Valerie, I had to win every inch of the ground. That being said, she claimed she liked it. She might have said something like, That French girl sure showed you the ropes, don't stop, I want it to go on. *Dicit.* So she said. *Sed mulier cupido quod dicit amanti, / In vento et rapida scribere oportet aqua.* We have seen the proof: What a woman says to a fervent lover should be written in the wind and rapidly flowing water. Yes, by then she knew about Jeanne. That I was for all practical purposes living with her. You're two-timing your mademoiselle! She'd laugh, most of the time. At other times, she'd say, Really, Hugo, it's unfair. If you like me as much as you say, you should tell her.

I had a good deal of trouble doing that, even though I agreed about the unfairness, and my postprandial sessions with Valerie were becoming something of a problem at the office. But I am ashamed to say that I liked sex with them both, or rather I liked sex with Jeanne better, but I needed my made-in-U.S.A. girl. And I was unable to behave better when I was in bed with Jeanne. In fact, my behavior was growing worse. There was only one way this thorny *vie en rose* could end. One afternoon, after she'd done with me, on her own initiative, something she assured me she had never done before, Valerie asked me to marry her. A good deal of bureaucratic deadweight had to be moved before that ceremony could be concluded in the *mairie* of the *huitième*. A wedding lunch followed, at Laurent, between avenue Gabriel and the Champs-Élysées. Henry Grunwald himself, my New York boss of bosses, attended. When Jeanne learned what I was doing, she slapped my face and told me I was a *beau salaud*. A real son of a bitch.

I finished my solitary meal at the Lipp. It seemed to me I had been at table forever. There were still a few diners left. Instead of calling for the check, I asked for a *poire*. A nostalgia trip, obviously. I hadn't had an *alcool blanc* since my days with Jeanne. Monsieur Gilles brought it to me himself and said it was a special bottle; I'd enjoy it. I invited him to sit down and have one with me, knowing full well that he would have to refuse. Broken, completely broken: that's how I felt. I had a second *poire*, paid the check, and staggered back to the hotel.

There was just enough energy, enough squeak left in me, as my mother might have said, left in me to call information and ask for Jacques Legrand's telephone number at the last address I had. That number was not in service. There was a subscriber corresponding to my indications, but at the subscriber's request the number was unlisted. Next, I went online and found a number of items. Obituaries of Jacques's mother and mother-in-law and several entries offering as a summer rental the house in Les Angles, near Avignon, that I was pretty sure he had sold some years earlier. And that was all.

I undressed and got ready for bed. Just as I was about to turn out the lights, a thought struck me. It was just possible that I had the email address of his daughter, a pediatrician last working somewhere in Africa, I couldn't remember where, for Doctors Without Borders. I searched contacts in my computer. There she was. I wrote asking for her parents' address and telephone number.

VIII

J ACQUES'S WIFE, LUCIE, answered when I rang the next morning.

It's really you, Hugo, are you in Paris, are you coming to spend the weekend with us, she cried in an explosion of delight that I hoped was unfeigned. Jacques will be *fou de joie*, so very happy! If you go straight to the Gare Saint-Lazare, you can catch a train to Bayeux and you'll be here in time for a late lunch. Or take a later train and come to dinner. Or take a train to Caen. Whichever you do, we'll pick you up at the station. Jacques didn't come to the telephone because he's out on a boat fishing. But he'll be home soon. Within the hour. Can he call you back?

When I stopped laughing I said I fully intended to go to see them but couldn't leave until Saturday morning, because I was busy with a conference at Sciences Po, that I still tried to avoid taking trains to travel relatively short distances, and that I'd been to Bayeux. For the tapestries, for the cemeteries, for I can't remember what else. I'd rent a car and if that was all right would be there for a late lunch tomorrow. And I'd stay until Sunday afternoon. But what are you and Jacques doing in Bayeux?

We sold Les Angles. You surely know that. After Jacques's mother died there was no real reason to hang on. Two of his uncles are still there—in two different nursing homes! Completely out of it. Meanwhile, everything anywhere near Avignon has gone up in value astronomically, and we sold the house for a fortune to some Brazilians who didn't seem to know or care how much they paid. Then we thought and thought about where we should go, and I said what about Bayeux? You've probably forgotten, but Jacques was the *sous-préfet* here years ago, and we still have links to the region and friends who haven't died—not yet. Jacques thought this was a great idea, and we were able to buy a charming little house in the old town. You'll see. We can walk everywhere, we don't have a big garden or a swimming pool to worry about, and we're very happy.

And Paris? I was genuinely astonished.

We sold that too, last spring.

Heavens! I said and looked at my watch. I'll want to hear all the details tomorrow, but now I've got to go to my conference. Give me your exact address and expect me tomorrow, no later than two!

There were probably garages nearer the hotel, but, because it felt like the old days, I made a reservation at the rental place on boulevard Raspail I had always used, picked up a car rather fancier than my Volvo, found I could still maneuver in the traffic on the *périphérique*, and hit A13 heading west. I had always liked French drivers. They're a little crazy and dangerous when drunk, but they keep out of the passing lane except when they want to pass. I found a station playing old-time jazz and cast my mind on happier days. At a quarter of two, with the help of the GPS, I was at Jacques's door. The house was narrow and beautiful, the façade meticulously maintained. When he opened the door, we threw our arms around each other. The underground garage was a couple of blocks away. I drove to it with Jacques but was grateful when he offered to take over and park the BMW for me. I have a dread of those places I find difficult to overcome.

Everybody changes. We note the irreparable outrage wrought by aging even when the faces and bodies belong to people we love and see daily. The passage of time between encounters—weeks, months, or even years—can make the effect shocking. I hadn't seen Lucie and Jacques since 2012 or 2013 and had preferred not to imagine how they might have been transformed. But they were much the same, once very blonde Lucie perhaps a little grayer, Jacques a tiny bit balder, both of them a little stouter, but I couldn't be sure of that, it could have been the effect of their country clothes, Lucie's face possibly plainer because she wore no lipstick, Jacques less closely shaved than when he was this or that minister's chief of staff. Nothing had changed in the imme-

diate flow of affection among us, Jacques's beautiful baritone voice calling out, It's about time, it's about time you
had come to check on us. The interior of the house was reas-
suringly familiar too, furniture I had known from Jacques's
and then Jacques and Lucie's successive apartments in Paris,
from their house in Les Angles, and his mother's house in
Villeneuve. The tension, sadness, and regret I had felt fell
away. I told Lucie that the effect they had on me was magical.

You shouldn't have stayed away so long, she said, and why
haven't you brought Valerie?

It couldn't be helped. I recounted my astonishment when
she let me know through her preposterous Irish lawyer
that she was leaving me, the quick-time march to divorce,
and the state of suspension in which I had been living
since then, between the city and Bridgehampton, somehow muddling through to the completion of my book on
Bush/Cheney. They expressed all the outrage I might have
expected. Jacques interrupted the outpouring to say, Your
book on Bill Clinton was most entertaining.

I was genuinely surprised. Like many, perhaps most,
French high civil servants of his generation, Jacques had
only an approximative if not comical knowledge of English.
Making his way through three hundred twenty pages of
my prose must have been his via crucis. He understood my
wordless reaction and laughed. Don't waste time pitying
me, I read you in French translation, you cretin!

Quite honestly, I had forgotten that a French translation
existed and congratulated Jacques on having bought one of

the thirty-six copies that had been sold. We returned to my new form of existence, and I assured my friends that I hadn't found a new love interest or companion and had no plans for reorganizing my life. Would I write another book after Bush/Cheney? I would first have to find a new subject. And no, I had no desire to travel. Really, I couldn't think of any place I would like to visit that I didn't already know. Unless it was my past. I was poking around in it. Apropos of visiting the past, I confessed that I had seen Jeanne and her husband.

That poor Jeanne! exclaimed Lucie. What a terrible life.

Of course, they had known her during my bureau chief days in Paris, just as they later came to know Valerie.

Terrible, but *tout confort,* every convenience. Jacques laughed. Hubert was handsome, very pleasant, great family, very rich, very social, Jockey Club, good job at an investment bank. Ha! A Viry, whose direct ancestor went to the Third Crusade, becomes a lickspittle in a Jewish bank! You must admit that's hilarious. Of course, they were only too happy to have him, and the job didn't interfere with his real passions, horses and hunting. It's awful what happened to him! She should have stayed with you!

That wasn't in the cards, I replied.

We never really liked Valerie!

During the walk Jacques and I took in Bayeux, over dinner, next morning while all three of us strolled in the American cemetery overlooking Omaha Beach, our talk centered on their lives, and I discovered I was basking in their happiness as a couple. Their one child, Sylvie-the-heroic-pediatrician, filled them with pride, although her adventures in Africa were often scary. There was a "young man" in the picture, a surgeon also attached to Doctors Without Borders, whom she was going to marry if they ever were together long enough in one place. As for Lucie and Jacques, they lived quietly, *sans histoires,* and comfortably, what with Jacques's pension, the proceeds of the sale of their overpriced real estate, and the small amounts of money they had inherited. They were in good health, the little tumor in Jacques's right lung having been shrunk out of existence by radiation and light chemo. Giving up Paris didn't turn out to be hard.

That's how I had hoped to live, that's how I thought I was living before Valerie left, I couldn't stop myself saying. I loved her, I'm sure I did, and I really thought she loved me, but it turned out I was a fool. Her departure shone a light that revealed me to be a fool and as counterfeit everything I had taken for granted as real and—how shall I put it?— good. Now I recognize the summum bonum, anyway for an old fuddy-duddy like me: a couple that's united by affection, I'm avoiding the word "love," and profound sympathy. I don't care, I added, whether it's a man or a woman or two men or two women. I know admirable queer couples. And now I really understand why I've been always drawn to certain people, why it wasn't unlikely in spite of my fundamental misanthropy that I'd become truly fond of them. They were part of a good couple. Just like you!

Jacques and Lucie were laughing. I'm glad we make a good impression, she said. Now let's hurry home. It's a thirty-minute drive from here to Bayeux and I want you to have a good lunch before your drive to Paris, if you really think you've got to go back today.

Later, when Jacques and I had a coffee near the garage from which, as promised, he was going to extract my BMW, he said it was bittersweet to hear my panegyric on Lucie's and his life together. Coming from you, it's almost comical. Think of all you've done: a crack foreign correspondent, head of two important overseas bureaus, and then the head of what was probably the best newsmagazine in the world, author of two books! And look at me: *sous-préfet* in this charming sleepy backwater who spent the rest of his career knocking about in the Ministry of Interior or the minister's office. I used to draw and paint, but I stopped. I tried to take it up again when we moved here. Zero. Our daughter, our wonderful Sylvie, might as well live on the moon. Lucie has never had an occupation other than her family, and she is totally uncomplaining. She plays tennis. I go out fishing with some locals. Lucie and I hold hands, old pal, and try to be brave. But we're no model for anything.

You're nuts, I told him. Had his English been stronger, I might have inflicted on him a few lines from "Lycidas": *Fame is no plant that grows on mortal soil, / Nor in the glistering foil / Set off to the world, nor in broad rumour lies, / But lives and spreads aloft by those pure eyes / And perfect witness of all-judging Jove...* Instead, I only hugged him once more and said I hoped he realized how happy seeing him and Lucie had made me.

———

I got into the car, set the GPS for boulevard Raspail in Paris, found the entrance to A13, and got going. The traffic was light. The radio station I had listened to on the way to Bayeux that played the jazz I like was still playing those same blues. I felt grateful and happy. Not more than forty-five minutes to my destination, I figured, a slightly less optimistic estimate than what the GPS calculated. Twenty-five minutes to Nanterre. The last time I'd been there it was to speak about the Clinton book. The time before last, on the tenth anniversary of the May events of 1968, in which Nanterre had played a not-insignificant role. The blessed radio station, whatever its name, had just begun my favorite, Fats Waller playing "Keepin' Out of Mischief Now," when everything went black.

I came to as I was being loaded on a stretcher into the ambulance. Out of the corner of my eye I saw the BMW squashed against the railing at the side of the road, the gendarmes, and a doctor or a medic in addition to the orderlies.

Really, I managed to squeak, I'm all right. Nothing the matter at all.

Don't try to speak, said the doctor type. Lie quietly. We'll check you out at the hospital.

The hospital was the Centre Hospitalier in Évreux, not much out of the way. A supermodern and efficient establishment, I thought. It was rapidly determined, in succession, that the alcohol level in my blood was no problem—not a surprise, since I had only two glasses of white wine at lunch, many hours earlier—that there was no internal bleeding, and nothing was broken, and that all the usual tests short of a CAT scan didn't reveal anything suspicious inside my skull.

You're very lucky, said the emergency-room doctor, a bossy woman I immediately liked. What do you think happened?

I blacked out. Lost consciousness. I have no other way to describe it.

Are you subject to fainting spells or vertigo?

I've never fainted in my life or suffered from dizziness, if that's what you mean.

Do you think you fell asleep?

No, I don't believe I did. I had a short nap before leaving Bayeux. I wasn't tired, and I didn't feel sleepy. It was just going black. Boom.

Has this sort of thing happened to you before?

Never while I was driving, I replied. It does happen when I am typing—I'm a writer and I spend a lot of time at my computer—and for instance while I'm reading the paper. It's not really falling asleep, I don't think. It's momentary loss of consciousness.

She looked puzzled. It may be narcolepsy. You should have it looked into by your doctor or perhaps a neurologist. Meanwhile, I think we should keep you here overnight. Just to make sure you don't get in trouble.

No, no, I exclaimed. That is quite impossible. I must get to Paris. I'll arrange for a car and driver to take me.

The thought that they might want to keep me in Évreux had begun to torment me. I could call Jeanne, explain the situation to her, and if necessary ask to put off our dinner until Tuesday. But what if she said she was busy, with those nephews, nieces, or whoever wanting to visit Hubert? If I were in a cast, if I required surgery, that would be another matter, but not in these circumstances.

The doctor was displeased. She shrugged and told me, I'm not going to keep you here against your will. But see a doctor—soon!

I didn't want to take the time to talk about it, but in fact I had seen one, my regular internist. He hadn't seemed particularly impressed—I had the feeling he took it as part of what you'd expect of an old jalopy like me with too many miles on it—but perked up when I mentioned the evenings during the reading period at college when one was hopelessly behind going through the novels on the French nineteenth-century-Romantics reading list and the only study aid that could possibly get one through, for instance, *Atala* was popping Dexedrine. What a pity, I said, that that miracle drug no longer exists. It does, it does, he replied, somewhat reformulated, under a different name. He prescribed it. Perhaps I had changed, perhaps the reformulation had been a mistake, I was left longing for the old stuff.

Leaving Évreux proved to be anything but simple. The

police had formalities to conclude, even though the case was simple—I'd blacked out and lost control of the car although not under the influence of alcohol—the rental company's local representative had paperwork as well.

To hell with discretion, I said to myself. I'll call Jacques. He used to fix my parking tickets in Paris; perhaps he can get me out of the clutches of these functionaries. I cut through his offers to come immediately to Évreux and take me home to Bayeux and similar well-intentioned proposals. I've got a date with Jeanne! I cried into the telephone. Please get me out of here.

There will always be a France, and a *sous-préfet,* even retired, will always have the ear of the police chief.

Lucie will kill me, he replied, but I'll do it.

I concealed as best as I could not feeling very steady on my feet, checked myself out of the hospital that fortunately accepted my credit card, and made my way across the street to a café that was still open. I ordered a crème, a ham-and-cheese sandwich on a buttered baguette, and called my hotel in Paris. The more intelligent of the night concierges was on duty. I explained I was stuck in Évreux without transportation. That I could try to take a train didn't occur to me. Could he send a car and driver? Should I try Uber? What did he recommend? He asked me to call back in ten minutes. Hallelujah! He had been able to reach a driver in Évreux itself, who would pick me up in a very short while. I remembered my overnight bag. It turned out that the orderlies had removed it from the back seat of the BMW. I picked it up and thanked my lucky stars.

The intelligent concierge was on duty when I arrived at the hotel, my bag in hand.

I beg your pardon, sir, he cried out, but what happened to you?

Why do you ask? I asked in turn. I was in a car accident, but I wasn't hurt. The doctors in Évreux examined me. If I look disheveled, it's because it has been a long and tiring day.

A bellboy appeared. The concierge told him to put my overnight bag in my room, and said, Really, Monsieur Gardner, please take a look in the mirror. He pointed to one next to the cashier's station.

I did as he told me. What I saw scared me. I understood why it had startled the concierge. I had deep black-and-blue half-moons under my eyes, the eyelids were black, and my eyes were bloodshot. Dark red. My hair was standing on my head. I smoothed it back.

Thank you, I said. Now I understand. These black-and-blue marks came out while I was in the car. We saw nothing like that when I was leaving the hospital.

Would you like me to ask the doctor to come over? We have a doctor in the neighborhood who is glad to take care of our guests.

Thank you again, I replied. These marks are scary, but I was checked thoroughly at the hospital and I am feeling fine, though hungry and tired. What I would really like is a pizza. Is the pizza place at the corner still open?

The concierge shook his head and telephoned without trying to hide his disapproval.

Yes, sir, it's open and they will be pleased to serve you if you come right over. By the way, the pizza is first-rate!

He was right about the quality of the pizza and I wondered whether he had not been right as well about the doctor. But no, I wouldn't change my mind. The crippling fatigue had to be considered normal. The same went for the aches and pains in every corner of my body. I had another glass of the heavy red wine and then yet another and understood with increasing clarity that the last thing I needed as a coda to my stay in Paris was involvement with the French health-care system, however excellent it had so far turned out to be. Quite simply, I had other things to do, the first and most important of which was the dinner with Jeanne. And she wasn't having dinner with me for my looks!

I took a sleeping pill and slept until almost ten when the need to urinate awakened me. On the way, I peeked in the mirror above the washbasin. If anything, I looked worse. Probably, I should have had ice compresses. But when?

In the ambulance? When I was being examined? In the
car on the way to the hotel? It was all nonsense. I rang for
my breakfast and the *NYT*. As I ate my brioche I concluded
that I was feeling much better. Really well. Ingrained habit?
I asked myself whether I should send Jeanne a bouquet
of tiny roses with some carefully unsentimental message.
For instance, *À ce soir*, followed by an exclamation point.
No signature. Then the absurdity of this project struck
me with full force. I went back to reading. Clinton and
Trump had debated the week before last in Saint Louis, and
they were to debate again tomorrow in Las Vegas. A suitable venue, I thought, for this bankrupt casino promoter.
The paper was full of speculation about the outcome of
these unlikely champions' final encounter. Would he knock
Hillary out? I wondered what he might do that was more
vile than bringing women Bill had allegedly molested or
abused to sit in the front row in the audience, or to threaten
to lock her up if he won the election. All I knew about Trump
told me he was a contemptible swine, and yet a significant
number of thinking and talking heads held that his performance on October 9 had saved his chances of winning
the White House. If that was true, if that was what voters
thought of his behavior, as a nation we had sunk to depths
of baseness not seen since the corrupt and racist presidency
of Andrew Johnson. Could Trump be elected? I was afraid
he could, running against a woman who couldn't come up
with one ringing, powerful reason why she should be president. What would I do, if it came to that? Why, nothing!

I wouldn't expatriate myself. There were a few Bonackers' houses on the north side of Route 27 in Bridgehampton and Sagaponack sporting ELECT TRUMP, TRUMP 2016, and MAKE AMERICA GREAT AGAIN signs, the rich folks on Gin, Lily Pond, Egypt, and Further Lanes being too discreet for any such display, but I had no doubt that the Hamptons and Manhattan were safe from the swine. That's where I would go to earth.

I dawdled over the paper and my laptop, and when I undertook to shave I discovered that however improved I might feel the circles around my eyes were larger and darker, the black and blue had spread down alongside my nose, my eyes were still bloodshot. I listened to myself carefully. No, I didn't have a headache. I stood first on one foot, then on the other, rose on my toes and was able to remain in position past the count of twenty. Doesn't look like a concussion, Dr. Hugo opined. I finished my toilet, took a hot bath, called Joséphine and made a dinner reservation, and went out to lunch. Another positive sign: I was beginning to be hungry. Lipp was out of the question. I wanted to avoid Monsieur Gilles's solicitous curiosity. Eager to test my physical condition, I walked to the Relais on avenue Montaigne, had a steak tartare and almost three-quarters of a bottle of the house Bordeaux, took a taxi back to the hotel, set my alarm clock, and went to sleep. At eight-twenty sharp, ten minutes early, I was at the restaurant, waiting for Jeanne.

IX

MY POOR DARLING HUGO, she cried out. Have you been mugged? What an awful beating!

I shook my head. She wore a black tuxedo I identified as the Saint Laurent number that had been the height of chic in the seventies and still looked great. She was made up with great care. One could now find in Paris hairdresser and barber salons open on Monday. Had she had a facial that afternoon? Because she was dining with me? Was the tuxedo an allusion to our time together?

Paris is still safe, I told her, at least in the *beaux quartiers.* No one beat me up. I'd been to Bayeux visiting Jacques and Lucie Legrand and yesterday evening on the way back I blacked out. Momentarily. I promise you I was one hundred percent sober. The car was totaled, and I was shaken up. That's all. If I only had the right masking cream, whatever you ladies use in such cases, I would have applied it.

How ghastly! Of course, you're lucky you weren't hurt. So, you went to visit Jacques and Lucie. I haven't seen them in a good while. They must have had a field day talking about me.

Not at all, I replied, they said they disliked Valerie and I should have stayed with you. About your husband: they said that before he became ill he was passionate about hunting, a fact I should have been able to deduce from the artwork on the walls of his room, and that he had been a banker.

Indeed. I'm sure they specified: a Viry working for Jews! That caused considerable hilarity in some milieus.

Jacques implied as much, in an offhand remark. Really, the part of our conversation that concerned you could not have taken up as much as three minutes. We talked about our lives. We hadn't seen each other for many years. The last time I was in Paris he was away, I don't know where. I've neglected him.

Just as you have neglected me!

I tried to protest, but she would not be stopped.

Then perhaps you don't know that Jacques has moved so far to the right he'll probably vote for Marine Le Pen. Of course, he's always been a frightful anti-Semite. I wonder how that squares with your very liberal politics.

You're right, I replied, I don't know any of that. We didn't discuss politics, not even the French election. Too many old war stories to occupy us. Hey, let's order a drink and our dinner.

While she pored over the menu, I remembered Jacques's habit of reducing trends in French society to apothegms, some of which I used to imagine were drawn from his expe-

rience at the Ministry of Interior and in the prefectural service, while others were the distillation of the worldview of
his winemaker uncles. One of his sayings was: *Le Français
est antisémite*, Frenchmen are anti-Semites. I argued with
him about that one, pointing out that he, for example, had
at least two very close Jewish friends I'd met through him.
Every anti-Semite does was his imperturbable reply.

She put down the menu, shaking her head, and said, I
really can't concentrate on this. I'll have whatever you're
having. Red wine, please, whether it's fish or meat.

I'll have what we used to like so much, I replied. Pea soup
and sautéed foie gras. All right? And a Saint-Estèphe?

Anything. Anything at all. I'm just thinking about how
conscious you are of having neglected your old pal Jacques.
And neglecting me? It doesn't even register on your emo-
tional scale.

Jeanne, I said, trying to choose my words carefully, you
were furious at me when I married Valerie, you said you
never wanted to hear from me or see me, and you were right
to be angry. I had behaved deplorably. You know that the
way we parted did not leave room for calling you when I
came through Paris and asking to have tea or a drink, or
for any other of those gestures one could expect when people have been so close. I made a huge mistake with Valerie,
for which I'm paying now, at a time in one's life when one
is most vulnerable. And I did you a wrong that I haven't
stopped regretting. Are you still so angry at me? Is that why
you seem so cross this evening?

To my horror, she began to weep, very silently, one tear after another running down along her nose, probably spoiling— I couldn't repress the thought—that perfect maquillage.

Jeanne, I whispered, Jeanne, really, I didn't mean to upset you.

She dried her face, took a deep breath, and said, It's all right, Hugo, you haven't upset me. It's the life I lead. I don't think you can conceive of what it's like. Just this evening: Monsieur le comte is running a fever! About six-thirty, after Hubert's evening Suze, Victor, I think that's the nurse who was on duty when you came to call, rushed in to see me and said, I saw that Monsieur le comte was flushed, and I took his temperature. The first time it was thirty-nine point five degrees. I've just taken it again and it's forty! Hugo, that's one hundred four Fahrenheit. Perhaps madame would like to call the doctor, Victor went on. Of course, I did. Fortunately, we have a doctor who lives and has his office on the rue du Bac and is willing to make house calls. Forty degrees! Hubert has so few opportunities to catch a virus—or anything! Only from those goddamn relatives. They could bring in the flu! Bubonic plague! AIDS! Joking aside, his having a high fever is really scary. The doctor came, and the usual awful circus began. Taking his temperature is easy, but you just try to find out whether he has any pain anywhere. The doctor says, Does this hurt? He takes that up and half speaks, half sings, Hurt! Hurt! Hurt! Hurt! On and on. The way he did with "Suze." You heard him. Not because he has any pain but because it's a word he can repeat. At least that's what we think. But perhaps he is in pain. It's hopeless. Can't find out whether there is any pain in his lungs. The poor doctor did what he always does. He took Hubert's blood and, just in case, gave him a shot of an antibiotic. He'll be back tomorrow.

That's awful. Terribly hard.

You can't imagine how hard. It's been going on for so long now and it will never stop. Dementia doesn't kill you. Inability to swallow does. An infection—that's what we're possibly dealing with now. High blood pressure and a stroke. Cancer. But Hubert appears to be in excellent health, and he certainly won't be run over by a bus or fall off a ladder or a horse.

I nodded. I really didn't know what to say. We ate in silence for a long moment. Then I found a question I could put.

What's your everyday life like, when there is no emergency? I asked. That too I find hard to imagine.

It's a desert, Hugo, a desert. Sometimes I think of Hubert and me as prisoners in a penal colony for two. What do I do? How do I spend my time? I make sure the household runs like clockwork. That takes some management. Someone who is no longer around to give me stupid helpful advice once asked, Why don't you hire a superbutler, to do it all? Why, indeed! First of all, they don't exist except on television. Second, if I found the superbutler I'd have to manage him! As it is, I manage the three male nurses, each doing an eight-hour shift, with an understudy who is always on call, plus the household personnel. Just in Paris that's four more people. And there is also our place in the Poitou, a beautiful house going back to Louis the Thirteenth that has had of course many things done to make it livable. My *notaire* and the accountant say I should sell it. I'm Hubert's guardian and sole heir, and I could put it on the market tomorrow, but the sister and her children would kick and scream. Kick and scream about what? Even if Hubert weren't demented he couldn't leave the château or his fortune to them. It's all locked up pursuant to the terms of our marriage contract. My father's *notaire* negotiated it with Hubert's *notaire,* but my father called all the shots. He has a real nose for business and for people. He got Hubert's number and yours too. He said, Don't trust *l'Amerloque,* he may think he likes you, but you're not his genre, he'll drop you like a used Kleenex. What he said about Hubert I won't repeat. As it turned out, Hubert didn't mind in the least disinheriting the sister and her children. We thought he got a kick out of it. He doesn't like them. You might ask, Why do they come and pay court if he can't do anything for them? Because they're dumb. The only way they'll get at Hubert's money is if I die first. They must think about that all the time. I wouldn't be surprised if they had me killed!

We had all but finished the bottle.

What wine is this? she asked.

Cos d'Estournel, I told her, 2009.

Can we have some more? If we have some cheese to go with it? Do you think that's reasonable?

That was more like the Jeanne I remembered. No, I told her, it isn't, but let's do it.

Anyway, I don't want to sell Poitou, she continued. It's where Hubert was happiest, and the nurses say he is still really happy when we move down there in the summer. I'm not sure that's right, or what his being happy means, but it's a nice idea. They take him into the rose garden. In the afternoon he sits on the terrace. Ever since he inherited the property from a Suze uncle, he's kept the hunt's hounds there, and pretty soon they made him master of the hunt. I had the hounds moved when he became really sick; it was ridiculous to keep them, but the nurses claim he sometimes makes baying noises and shakes his head, wondering, wondering. The season for hunting the *chevreuil*, roe deer, opens around September fifteenth. We always stay until the first week of October, sometimes until the fifteenth, because when Hubert is in residence the hunt rides over to our house. They form a semicircle in the courtyard and the horns sound the calls that the huntsman, an old servant whom Hubert always treated like a brother, remembers that Hubert liked the most. You know, "Les Honneurs," "La Saint-Hubert." It's stirring and really beautiful and I couldn't deprive Hubert of that.

You're so generous, I murmured.

Nonsense! The cost of the upkeep is not a problem. Hubert is really rich, and one day I probably will be rich too. If my idiot brother doesn't run the business into the ground after Father dies. It's the bother of keeping the show on the road when the show may not make any sense at all to the audience. I mean, one can't possibly tell what goes on in Hubert's head. The utter futility. For instance, how is one to tell whether he can distinguish *La Saint-Hubert* from "*La Marseillaise*"? And my unspeakable loneliness!

When it came to eating and drinking this was indeed the old Jeanne. We had a plum tart after the cheese. By the time our coffee was served, we had finished the wine.

Shall we have a cognac? I asked. There is so much more I'd like to know.

I want to tell you everything, but why don't we have the cognac at home?

I concealed my surprise and delight and was about to ask the waiter to call a taxi when she said, It's all right, my car is outside.

Indeed, it was. The man in a black suit who opened the door when I came calling now also wore a black chauffeur's cap. Once we were on the way, Jeanne moved over close to me and took my hand.

I want you to come home with me, Hugo, I want to get drunk with you, but nothing will happen. It won't be like our first time together. You know it can't be.

The huge apartment was dark and silent. "The grave's a fine and private place," I mused, "but none, I think, do there embrace." She led me to the library and pointed to the sofa. I took it that was where I was to sit down. I'll be right back, she whispered.

The man in a black suit, minus the cap, appeared, announced in sepulchral tones Delamain XO '61, and poured my drink. A sniff told me it was remarkable. I put the glass down on the coffee table and waited. Some long minutes passed—ten? fifteen? I hadn't looked at my watch—and Jeanne came, or rather glided, into the room. The man in the black suit followed and poured her drink.

That will be all, Georges, she said. You may leave the bottle on the coffee table. I will let out Monsieur Gardner myself and turn out the lights.

She had changed. She was wearing a black two-piece sweat suit and ballet slippers.

You're surprised. She laughed. I can still get into my old vintage clothes, like that smoking, but they're not really comfortable. Of course, they never were. In that respect, I'm lucky. I've pretty much kept my shape. Gym, more gym, and when we still kept horses, riding. I could have joined or followed the hunt, but I've never been able to bear running down and killing those poor little beasts and letting hounds devour them. Have you tried the cognac?

I waited for you.

No need to wait any longer. She slid closer to me on the sofa, raised her glass, and touched mine. It's wonderful, don't you think?

Yes, I managed to say. The heat of her body was very strong.

Well, have another sip. We have the whole bottle to keep

us company! You know, you can find out about my shape
yourself. Go ahead. There is nothing under this suit. Just
remember: it will not be like New York.

Was it not having had children? All that exercise? Considering how well she liked to eat and drink, extraordinary
metabolism? Her body was indeed astonishingly the same,
and as in the past everything moved astonishingly fast. She
spread her legs. I knelt down between them and pulled
down her pants. The orgasm came with the speed and force
of a bullet train. Let her rest, let her rest, I thought, and for
some minutes only caressed with my hand her thighs, buttocks, and belly. When I put my mouth on her again another
orgasm followed, slower but longer, and I thought more
pleasurable. Again, I let her rest, but this time she took hold
of my ears and very gently pulled me up.

Now you sit down, she said, it's my turn. She pulled off
her suit top, told me to let my trousers down and to nestle
between her breasts. At last, she took me in her mouth.

Come up here now, she ordered, and be very quiet. That
door—she pointed—leads to a bathroom, when you want to
wash.

Jeanne, I whispered, why don't you take me to your bed?
I am inordinately happy now, but we could be even happier.
Please!

She shook her head. I don't want to. This is what I wanted.
You liked it too. Don't be a glutton. Doing more might give
us more immediate pleasure, but it would leave me very
unhappy.

I washed my face, put my clothes in order, and went back into the library. She had disappeared but, as I expected, returned moments later, her hair combed, her eyes bright.

You are my darling Hugo, she told me, I'm very, very happy you've come to see me.

Then we're friends again?

Of course, you idiot. How could it be otherwise?

Then I have an idea. You say your life is very lonely. So is mine. How would it be if I took a little apartment in Paris, someplace not far from here, and we kept each other company? Nothing heavy or constraining. Just having someone who is your old friend you can talk to, who would take you to the opera or concerts or for long walks. And, from time to time, make out on a sofa like a pair of teenagers! Only I don't think teenagers do oral sex!

You're so old-fashioned, darling Hugo! Now teenagers all do it. But probably the answer has to be no. It would be too artificial. You don't belong in Paris, not without a job, and you're too old to get a job. I do have a job, a full-time job— looking after Hubert and running his house—and it's a job that takes priority. There would be fatal imbalance between us. You'd end up being bored and thinking you'd made a stupid deal. Please don't argue. Don't spoil it. I need a cognac, and so do you, and I want to be in your lap and in your arms.

I did as she said, and once again we drank to each other.

Aren't you going to caress me? she complained.

I put my hand under her top. Her nipple stiffened. That's better, she told me.

Jeanne, I said, Hubert has been sick for such a long time, is it possible that your husband-and-wife life, I mean sex, has continued?

What a dope you are—she laughed—don't stop what you're doing, and I'll tell you all about it. You know, not all men are like you, always wanting to jump into bed and so on. Not very long after I married Hubert, sometime after we found out that he couldn't have children, he'd had mumps or something, I realized that I was a secondary interest. His real passion was horses, and once in a while a groom. Don't misunderstand me. He wasn't a committed queer. Anyway, never a lasting relationship. Also, he'd still ask to sleep with me. Infrequently. That's all. When he'd gotten excited about something that wasn't necessarily me. These occasions, I have to say, weren't memorable. I'd need to prepare him. He never managed to get it up without help. Sometimes a lot of help. Then, I'd open my legs, he'd do his thing, and that was that. I always made sure I had enough lubricant on hand. He never prepared me! Strictly a one-way street. He'd always snored, but it seemed the snoring got worse and worse until one night I recorded the concert and played it for him in the morning. He was appalled and apologized over and over. That's one thing you have to understand about Hubert. He is truly polite. That may have something to do with his being so easy to deal with now. Anyway, that gave me the justification I needed to say that we really had to have separate bedrooms. He didn't object, and the conjugal visits took on a ceremonial quality that wouldn't have been out of place at the court of Louis the Fourteenth. So that's the family life of Madame la comtesse de Viry! Just what she had hoped for.

Like that, all those years! How have you been able to bear it?

Do that some more, she murmured.

I had been squeezing first one nipple, then the other.

No, she said, at some point, it seems like an age ago, I took a lover. I mean really long ago. Let's say thirty years. A real old-fashioned lover, with a garçonnière, great style, great distinction. Same age as you or a couple of years younger. Moving in the best French society. If I told you his name, you'd recognize it instantly. You may even know him. Of course, he was married, of course his wife was extremely religious, going to mass every morning, and of course wouldn't dream of giving him a divorce. And of course, she knew about us, but that changed nothing. Hubert knew too. It was hardly a secret in our milieu and I'm shocked that Jacques didn't tell you about it. Perhaps he isn't as well connected as he thinks. It was a good arrangement. Did it make me happy? "Happy" is such a difficult word. I think it did until one fine day, about six years ago, when he ditched me. Just like that, just the way you ditched me, darling Hugo, and took up with someone we all know who is thirty years younger!

I was going to say, What a cad, but thought better of it and, reaching for a neutral comment, said, That's quite a story. Good plot for an eighteenth-century comedy.

It gets better, she said. A couple of years ago the young beauty dumped him for a Russian billionaire! A married Russian billionaire! Can you imagine it? Giggling, she slid off my lap. In the next gesture, she shed her sweatpants and said, Hugo, my love, do again what you did before.

She did not offer to return the favor, and I did nothing to encourage such a project. I wasn't sure it would work. She asked for some cognac and reproved me when I only poured a drop into my glass. I wasn't drunk, but I thought I was reaching the point at which my balance when I undertook to walk might be in question. Jeanne was purring in a way that made me think she was beautifully tipsy.

Perhaps I should leave, I said. You've made me very happy. Happier than I've been in a very long time.

That was quite true.

By way of answer, she kissed me on the mouth. Then she told me she was happy too. Happy and content.

Do you think you'll come back? she asked.

Do you mean tomorrow? Before I leave Paris? Shall I extend my stay? Will you allow me to go through with my plan? I've always wanted to have a garçonnière!

No, darling Hugo, she said, I can't say yes to that, not tonight, I really meant what I said before. I wanted to know whether you will come to Paris again, before so many years pass?

Yes, I replied, often. In a couple of months. Sooner if you change your mind. And now I must go.

I turned down her offer to summon a radio taxi. The night

was clear and windless. I took the rue de Solférino to the boulevard Saint-Germain, followed it to rue Bonaparte, and followed rue Bonaparte to rue Cassette and my hotel. I did not feel any too steady on my feet, but remembering not to shuffle, I managed not to stumble and fall. There was a Georges Moustaki song Jacques Legrand used to sing obsessively in his fine baritone voice during our long drives to the country, before the autoroute drastically cut the travel time to Avignon. The refrain came into my mind and I began to hum it: *il est déjà demain, passe, passe le temps, il n'y en a plus pour très longtemps....*

X

I AWOKE LATE, went to the bathroom, looked at my scary face, and saw I was smiling. I felt like hell, but I was smiling, and the smile remained on my face while I ordered my breakfast and ate it and even as I recalled that Hillary's and Trump's third and final debate would take place that evening in Las Vegas. Starting at eight, New York time, I supposed, therefore at two in the morning in Paris. Never mind. I'd watch it. But I couldn't concentrate on Hillary or Trump. I thought about Jeanne and me. *Les aiguilles ont tourné*, the hands on the clock have turned, in the words of Moustaki's song. It was already past eleven. I had little time to lose.

I dressed rapidly, took a cab to place du Palais-Bourbon, and studied the florist's window. I wanted to send Jeanne a plant. The orchids were particularly beautiful. With the help of the owner, whom I had known as a very young woman learning the trade at that very store, I picked a five-stem specimen, its petals a Niagara of white. A perfect plant, the owner assured me, in full bloom but with many buds waiting to open. A card had to go with it. I knew what to say: *Merci!* Underneath I drew a smiley face. That was the sort of thing Jeanne used to like. I hoped she still did. Does madame know how to take care of orchids? I hadn't seen any in my brief walk through the apartment. Georges the man in the black suit probably did. To be on the safe side, I had the owner add instructions: plenty of light, but no direct sunlight, water once a week, direct sunlight once the petals have fallen, if all goes well the plant will flower again. Could the plant be delivered soon? *À l'instant même, Monsieur Gardner.*

I'd had breakfast, but I felt ravenous. There was a restaurant next door to my former hotel on rue de Bourgogne. While I ate lunch there, a plan formed in my head. The first step was to look at the Degas at the Musée d'Orsay. I had a mental list of favorites: the two canvases of bathers drying their feet, all the café portraits, the bronzes of young dancers, the dance class. They would take me into the world of Maupassant, Zola, Mallarmé, Renoir, and Monet, a world I loved, its horrible politics and injustice notwithstanding. A moment at which, before the Dreyfus Affair and the painter's anti-Semitism irremediably estranged them and set that world on a path to disappearance, Degas would paint time and time again members of the Halévy family who treated him as one of their own. I didn't know how many of these paintings could be seen. They might be away, on loan. There were others. I wouldn't be choosy. The second step was to arrange to go to Vienna tomorrow, in the late afternoon—if I was going to watch the debate, I would be even less eager than usual to rise early. The third was to call Jeanne.

I telephoned just before six. I took that to be the hour of Hubert's Suze, a ceremony I supposed she attended. I was ready to confront the redoubtable Georges, but, once again, she answered herself.

Darling Hugo, she cried, that is the most beautiful orchid plant, no, orchid tree, no, orchid forest I've ever seen. Do you know that Hubert never sent me flowers? And my lover claimed to be a minimalist. The most he could do consistent with his aesthetic was a bunch of violets or forget-me-nots or, all winter long, pompons. He claimed that showed true refinement. It showed me he was a cheap son of a bitch.

Had she had a glass of champagne too many preparing herself for the ordeal of the Suze, for how else could one think of it, or had our evening together and speaking to me liberated her, loosened her tongue so strangely? I felt immense tenderness and sympathy for her. Did I love her these many decades ago? Was I falling in love? These were questions I couldn't for the moment answer.

I have a great weakness for orchids—in all their variety, I told her. I'm happy you like this one. Are you by any chance free tonight? If you are, and if you're game, we could have a late dinner together and then watch awful Hillary debate the ten times more awful Trump. The debate will start late. Two in the morning. But I think it will be worth it.

Darling Hugo, I can't, I can't possibly! The dreaded sister and two of the dreaded children are coming to dine in state with their uncle Hubert. By the time they leave I will be ready for bed—ready to go to bed alone.

That is too bad. I'm leaving for Vienna in the late afternoon. Back on Sunday evening. Do you think you might be free for dinner?

Yes, yes, yes! Will you stay in Paris after that?

Perhaps. It will depend only on you, *ma petite* Jeanne. I do have to be back in New York for an appointment I mustn't miss on Monday, the thirty-first, and of course I want to be there to vote.

I see, she replied, and I could imagine her pouting, that doesn't give us much time.

And then, brightening, she added, Could we have lunch tomorrow, before you take your plane?

Chez Lipp, I replied, at one-thirty. It's not impossible that once again you're making me lose my head.

Making my Vienna arrangements turned out to be a cinch. The combination of the Internet—thank you, Al Gore, for inventing it—and the smartphone have made dizzyingly easy the sort of thing that would have required endless conferences with the concierge of a five-star palace, and a hefty tip to that potentate, or a tiresome visit to the American Express travel office or some other haven for tourists with unshaved legs squatting on the floor beside their backpacks. Yes, there was a direct flight from Paris to Vienna in the late afternoon and I could have a seat in the business class, yes, the reservations clerk at Hotel Sacher remembered me not only from my most recent stay when I was promoting the Clinton book but also from the many prior stays in my earlier avatars, and, yes, so did the concierge. That functionary saw no reason why he couldn't get tickets for me to see *Eugene Onegin* and *Le nozze di Figaro*. The Internet had already informed me that *Les Troyens* and *Un ballo in maschera* were also on that week, and I asked him to substitute *Les Troyens* for one of my first choices if absolutely necessary. Finally, he assured me I could have a table at the hotel's Rote Bar every evening of my stay; as soon as I was ready tomorrow after my arrival at the hotel, at eight-thirty if I wasn't going to the opera; and otherwise after the performance.

It was, in fact, at the Rote Bar, while I sipped my second perfect gin martini and listened to the piano player work his way through "Parlez-moi d'amour," that the bizarre sensation of apprehension and disgust I experienced watching Clinton and Trump returned to me. He would not commit to accept the result of the election? Took that position not just once but twice, perhaps three times? He'd keep us in suspense! Called his opponent a nasty woman! A woman who shouldn't be allowed to run for the presidency? Why wouldn't he say that and anything else that came into his mind? After all, he'd declared that if he were elected president, he'd appoint a special prosecutor to go after her, and in Florida called for her to be locked up. The press I read online led me to believe that my erstwhile colleagues had concluded that by his performance in the debate Trump had driven a nail into his coffin, probably had nailed it shut. If only they turned out to be right! As usual at about ten in the evening every table at the Rote Bar had been taken. I looked around the room at what seemed to me in great majority Viennese bourgeois sniffing the good Blaufränkisch red in balloon glasses, smacking their lips at the *Tafelspitz* set out on the plates before them, and studied their double-breasted black or pinstriped navy-blue suit jackets, the cut of which had not changed much from what their fathers or grandfathers might have worn seated in this very bar a couple of weeks after the Anschluss, so many of them secretly or not so secretly glad to be rid of weaklings like Dollfuss, Schuschnigg, and Miklas and proud to be at last part of the greater Reich. In 1932 people like me and those colleagues of mine who thought that Trump had been walloped considered Hitler and the garbage he spewed ridiculous, preposterous, absurd. Then, bingo, he very legally won the election, and war hero President Hindenburg very legally named him chancellor. The United States isn't anything like the Weimar Republic, and analogies are almost always false or useless, I told myself, and took comfort in that thought and in the goulash that had just arrived steaming on my plate. And in the very dry Tokay I had ordered after a lengthy consultation with the sommelier. All things considered, it was difficult not to think that the Austro-Hungarian Empire was a better arrangement than the emerging concert of Eastern Europe's neofascists. The room had thinned out. The piano player, who like everyone else at this hotel seemed to remember me or the generosity of my tips, came to my table, inquired after my health without letting on that he'd noticed the black-and-blue rings around my eyes, and asked whether there was a piece I would like to hear. I was just then thinking about Jeanne. All right, the request was corny. I asked him to play "I've Got You Under My Skin."

Kunsthistorisches Museum—Emperor Franz Joseph's fabulous gift to his people of the building and the imperial collections. Only the Prado is a comparable example of royal generosity. As always in Vienna when I wasn't working, right after breakfast I followed Ringstrasse to the museum. Once there, I went from Brueghel to Vermeer, from Vermeer to my favorite Giorgione, *Laura,* from her to Cranach's *Judith with the Head of Holofernes.* It doesn't take long before I get what I call museum eyes—when I see but don't see. That is the time to leave. I took a cab to Demel, expanded but otherwise unchanged since I first went there as a soldier on leave. After a lunch composed of marvelous little sandwiches, I walked to the Albertina. I had a specific goal in mind, those Schiele drawings that are not in the Leopold Museum. Leopold was where I intended to spend the next afternoon. Why Schiele? Because of the mixture of contentment I felt at being in Vienna and anxiety about the decade that lay ahead. Not that I particularly expected to see it through. It was enough to have it there, its hot fetid breath like that of a devouring beast. Schiele's skeletal nudes, their crazed eyes, cavernous mouths, and shamelessly exposed pudenda, his self-portraits, were all surely portents of what lay ahead, of upheavals that would have defied even his imagination. He was lucky. His wife and he died of the Spanish flu a few short weeks before the Great War ended. He did not witness those upheavals. Had they been portents as well of what was to come now, as a new darkness was descending on us?

I believed every word of *Le nozze*, even Barbarina's adorable *L'ho perduta, me meschina*... her lament over the loss of Susanna's pin. As always, I shook my head in puzzlement at Onegin. Could there be a young man callous and obtuse enough to fail to accept the love that Tatiana offered? And I hastened to assure myself that there was no commonality between my treatment of Jeanne and his spurning of that adorable romantic Russian maiden. Both evenings, my seat was in the first row of a grand tier box, and both evenings the other seats were occupied by voluble Austrians who had filled all the places except mine and ignored me except for the occasional complaint about the inconvenience of my presence. They were apparently convinced I didn't understand or speak German and I didn't think I'd make myself or them feel better by letting them know they were mistaken. They too were elegant bourgeois types, the men dark suited and well barbered, the women in black, blonde or very gray, three strands of pearls and pearl earrings completing the perfect picture. If the rise of the far right, standing on the brink of sharing power with the establishment, and the migrant crisis were portents, they left these good people undisturbed. Tatiana, meanwhile, had reached the end of her wrenching final aria, leaving Onegin bowed and without hope. The curtain came down, the applause was frenetic, and I was momentarily transported to the Metropolitan Opera. It occurred to me that, if I were in New York, I might be there this very evening. How much angst would I perceive on the faces of my fellow bourgeois New Yorkers, those who like myself had watched Clinton debate Trump?

On Saturday, my last evening in Vienna, I had dinner with a much-younger colleague, once a political reporter and now an editorialist for the Vienna *Kurier* who had become a friend. We worked together on the Kurt Waldheim affair in 1986 and '87, the furor over the undisclosed or indeed concealed facts relating to his military service as an intelligence officer in a German unit that committed war crimes in the Balkans culminating in his being declared persona non grata by the United States even though he was the incumbent president of Austria and had served two terms as secretary-general of the United Nations. Among the piquant or troubling aspects of that sorry business was the indifference of a solid majority of the Austrian public to what it learned about Waldheim's past, the possibility that the intelligence services of the United States, the United Kingdom, the Soviet Union, and Israel had closed their eyes to it when he became a candidate for the United Nations office, and the surge of anti-Semitism in Austria provoked by the aggressive role played by the World Jewish Congress in bringing Waldheim's wartime service into the open. We recalled this bizarre story over smoked trout, *Tafelspitz*, Wiener schnitzel, *Kaiserschmarrn*, and abundant Sangiovese my friend wrinkled his nose at my suggesting an Austrian red.

Nodding half solemnly, he said, It's quite a little country, my beloved Austria. We haven't had it so good since Franz Joseph, but we're split right down the middle. No, right down the middle may be an exaggeration. But almost half of us would like to bring the Reich back. The Reich without war, but also without Turks, migrants, all other polluters of our soil. You're lucky to live in the U.S. Because Clinton will beat that clown. That's very clear, isn't it?

That's what the polls tell us, I replied. I hope they're right.

I had put my cell phone on mute while we were in the Rote Bar. Back in my room, I discovered I had a message from Jeanne. You can call me back as late as you like. And she left her own cell phone number, which I hadn't previously known.

It was eleven-thirty, not an indecently late hour. Anyway, if she had gone to bed, it would be in her own bedroom. She answered immediately. *Enfin, c'est toi.*

I told her I'd finished dinner with an Austrian journalist pal talking about the times when we worked together. Toward the end, he got very serious, worried about the rightward drift of Austrian politics. Clearly, she wasn't interested.

Hugo, she said, I understand that you have to vote in the election. That's November eighth. I just checked. Why do you have to go back before November seventh? Why won't you stay in Paris?

My love, I told you that I need to be in New York on October thirty-first. It's an appointment I really mustn't miss. It's not for fun, it's not what I really want to do. It's something I have to do.

I could hear the pout forming on her lips.

And you won't tell me what it's about?

It's a long, tiresome, and unpleasant story. Certainly not one you want to hear about over the telephone when you should be going to sleep.

I realized I was striking the wrong note, but I didn't know how to do better.

Very well. And when do you get back to Paris tomorrow?

If the traffic is no worse than usual, I should be at my hotel by eight.

Then please let's have dinner tomorrow at nine.

Joséphine? I asked.

It may be closed on Sunday. Let's have dinner chez Lipp. It's close to your hotel. And please think again about that mystery appointment. Is it really necessary?

Of course, it wasn't necessary. Keeping watch over my prostate could wait. I could call Dr. Klein and tell him I was stuck in Europe, or tied up in Europe if not marooned, and would he please reschedule me. Did I really care what those cells were doing? If they were doing nothing, or simply multiplying tranquilly inside that gland, why that was nice. If they had actually broken out and were marching to positions to be taken up in this organ or another, that was far less nice. There was an intermediate possibility too, that still inside that wretched gland they had multiplied to such an extent that the good doctor would declare the invasion imminent. If they were quiescent, everything was simple: we do nothing. In the two other cases, he'd doubtless want me to start treatment. Radiation was a good bet. It was also a good bet he'd say the chances of its leading to incontinence were close to zero or perhaps zero and that its leading to impotence was a possibility. That led to interesting questions: Did I care? Would Jeanne care—assuming for the sake of argument that, all other things considered, she would like to have me back on some part-time basis—and I was willing to become her "monsieur" making love to her on her library sofa or at the garçonnière I would acquire? Did making love need to include erection and penetration? If my most recent experience held a lesson, very likely it didn't. The blow job she so beautifully gave me was, I thought, almost surely intended to give me pleasure. All the deep-throat stuff notwithstanding, I couldn't believe it did much for her. That analysis if it led anywhere might lead to the conclusion that since protecting my precious ability to get a hard-on was not an absolute necessity—and, by the way, how long would that ability continue even absent radiation—I should by all means keep my appointment and make sure those cells were properly checkmated. But there was a voice that could not be stilled whispering that all this is nonsense, the real cure is not the X-ray machine but whatever the ultimate doctor, the one I would call upon in Zurich, would instill in my veins.

There was a single malt whiskey in the minibar. I drank it and the provisional solution emerged. I would have as happy a time as possible over the next couple of days with Jeanne and I would keep my end-of-the-month appointment. What was the reasoning behind it? I don't think I knew.

I called ahead and reserved chez Lipp, not because I lacked confidence in Monsieur Gilles's goodwill but because I didn't want to impose on it, not on Sunday, at the busiest hour. When Jeanne arrived, he brought her to my table with a smile of deep satisfaction, executed a little bow, and murmured, My respectful greetings for Monsieur le comte.

Hubert came here all the time, she explained, offering me her lips. This time she wore a black dress with a full skirt that I didn't think was Saint Laurent. Valentino—she laughed—when he was still good.

I felt unutterably happy to be with her.

It took very little time, however, for the logistics of ordering dinner, the sense of peace that descends with the first champagne and gin martini, to recede as Jeanne returned to the need for me to keep my appointment. I had thought she would, and had decided I wouldn't equivocate. I told her, as best and as dryly as I could, the nature of the appointment, the condition that had made it advisable, and how I had most recently thought about it in relation to what was happening between her and me. Once again, I saw tears run down along her nose. She cried noiselessly.

Jeanne, I whispered, I beg of you, stop. I'm an old man. Don't take a tragic view of this stuff. I don't. I've spoken at your insistence and in order to be fair.

Yes, she said. You were right to speak. I will speak too. It's not necessary for you to be able to get it up. It is necessary for you to want to live, and to want to be with me on the only terms that are now possible.

The rest of the evening—the part played out on her sofa—and the following evenings were weirdly like the first evening except that she was even more passionate. There was a difference the night before my departure. She asked me to take her, to come inside her.

Here? I asked. You want me to undress here? No, she

whispered back, don't undress, just let your trousers down, I want to feel them rough on the inside of my thighs.

I was lucky. I was able to perform. She lay in my arms afterward, her breasts, she said, aching to be caressed.

I sent her another orchid the next morning, one that I thought was even more magnificent, but I didn't ask her to have lunch with me. I thought that if I saw her I might lack the strength of will needed to get myself on the plane.

XI

I**T WAS NOT UNPLEASANT** to be back in the city, to have lunch at our club with Rod, to catch up on Mrs. Perez's troubles with her carpenter husband who, despite all the demolition and rebuilding of apartments in the city, seemed to be out of work every other week. I was secretly grateful to the husband's bosses for not keeping him fully employed. That was the only reason, I felt certain, why Mrs. Perez's own working habits were exemplary unless her extravagant end-of-the-month troubles interfered. Rod reported a pickup in his firm's and his own billable hours. That was very good news. Nonetheless, Carla was urging him to take a position being dangled before him of general counsel for the U.S. at the biggest Dutch insurance company, with a clear shot at a higher management position. It would be an immediate pay cut, but his income would rise each year, it wouldn't depend on ups and downs in the M&A market, and the benefits including his eventual pension were unbeatable. I was grateful for these positive if not brilliant developments in Rod's professional life and, above all, for his not needing to keep a stiff upper lip when we got together. He asked me what I thought. I told him the truth, that I had always rather liked the buccaneer side of a lawyer's life, being one's own master, and so forth, but feared that the image in my head was sadly out of date. If that was ever true or somewhat true, and anyway if what that image implied did not correspond to what he really wanted, then, if I were him, I'd let myself be influenced by Carla's advice. She's a very smart girl, I added.

As I spoke, I realized I was a bore. A crashing bore. Perhaps right there was the root reason my relations with the children were what they were. But I couldn't help it. As Valerie would have said, I was born that way. Miraculously, Rod didn't seem to mind. He nodded, very seriously, and told me I was right on both points. There was a lot to be said for saying hail and farewell to his dear partners and becoming a client. This encouraged me, and I ventured a question. How is Barbara? You and she must be in touch.

Who knows? he answered. She and the doctor are fighting a lot. That's what one of the girls told Carla.

I walked him to Grand Central, where he took his subway. I caught a taxi. I would be fifteen minutes or so early for the bloodletting that preceded my appointment with the urologist, but that was all right. I could while away the time reading something instructive, like *Men's Health*. I had hit the nail right on the head in my cogitations. The gland is larger, Dr. Klein told me, though still not hard, and it's good you have no symptoms. Let's wait for the PSA results. We'll have them for you next Monday. That's the seventh. One day before the election. Let's hope we'll like them, and that we will be able to like what we'll find out the next day! I look forward to seeing you then!

When I got home I discovered that Jeanne had taken to using email. The message from her read: What happened? *Je t'adore.*

Ten-thirty in the evening in Paris. She sent her email at ten. Surely, she was alone. I called her cell-phone number. It must have been on her night table—for some reason, I assumed she had gone to bed—I didn't think it had rung before she answered.

Tell me what happened, darling Hugo! I've been very anxious all day.

Nothing much, I told her. The usual. We need to see what the bloods show us. The doctor said, Come to see me in a week and we'll discuss. Really, Jeanne, don't worry about any of this. It's as I told you. All the outcomes are possible, and I'm ready to accept whichever one it is.

You are, she fired back. I'm not. No one who cares for you can be.

I apologized at once for what I called my excess of dryness and said if she wanted to worry about something really worrisome it was right there, staring us all in the face. That's the election in the U.S.

You are *vraiment con*, a real idiot, she replied, and hung up.

There was another message in my email in-box, from

Mark and Edie Horowitz. Please call! We're giving an election-night party. You need to come!

A three-alarm Texas chili was on the bill of fare at the Horowitzes', the guests no different from what I expected. Mark enveloped me in a bear hug and shouted over the din, At the last party like this over here you and I were sick to watch that monster Ted Cruz declare his candidacy. We don't have to worry about him anymore. How well Boehner put it: Lucifer in the flesh! And after tonight we won't have to worry again about that Orange Clown. Dustbin of history!

He reflected, I said to myself, the editorial convictions of the *NYT,* his old mother ship, and I saw something of the same confidence in the faces all around me. We had come to watch a coronation. One that progressed slowly and prosaically until each battleground state fell into place and Hillary's headquarters in Brooklyn would erupt in uncontrollable joy. Perhaps because I disliked both Clintons and had found Hillary unconvincing as a candidate, unless you took a woman's becoming president to be a sufficient reason in itself, perhaps because thoughts about my personal situation had soured me, I found I was out of sync with my fellow diners and drank more than usual to find and maintain the proper distance from what CNN was reporting. Relatively early, I don't think it was much later than ten, Wisconsin and Michigan were called for Trump. I didn't need to hear more. So far as I was concerned, he had won the election, and I didn't stick around to hear poor John Podesta acknowledge defeat on his candidate's behalf, or the insinuations that the candidate was too drunk to speak for herself, or Trump's hypocritical victory speech.

I went home, poured myself a huge bourbon that I decided to drink neat, and reread the email I had sent Jeanne the evening before.

My love, I had written, as the French like to say, *rien n'est simple et tout se complique,* nothing is simple, and everything gets balled up. The doctor said that my PSA—that's an indicator revealed by the blood test—is "off the charts." That means to him that it's way too high. It doesn't mean that the cancer cells have moved from the prostate gland to other organs. In these circumstances, the doctor says he can't any longer agree with my decision to choose "watchful waiting" over treatment. Treatment would consist of an intensive course of radiation. What does intensive mean? The radiologist specializing in cancers of the prostate would make that decision. Dr. Klein thinks it would probably mean five days a week or perhaps six days a week sessions over four to six weeks. He'd like the treatment to start right away. Incontinence, he assures me, is not a risk. Impotence resulting from the radiation cannot be excluded.

If I'm not a good boy, don't have the treatment, and the cancer spreads, it may well spread in ways that cannot be cured by surgery or with any degree of assurance of obtaining a cure by radiation or chemotherapy. These cancers that have traveled, he warned me, are often excruciatingly painful and do not always respond well to painkillers. Of course, he'd like to take a look inside me in the next couple of days to see what if anything is going on now.

You mean you want a trip down Rectum Boulevard? I had asked, thinking I'd get a laugh out of him. I didn't. He asked, rather crossly, whether his secretary should make an appointment for me with the radiologist.

I'll have to think about it, I told him. May I let you know?

What's there to think about? the good doctor asked me, comically shocked.

My reply was a smile and a Churchill victory sign.

As you know, my love, I've been giving this dreary business a good deal of thought and it didn't take me long to reach a decision. The decision is that no, I will not undertake the treatment.

Hear me out, darling Jeanne, these are my reasons.

1. The cancer may or may not spread, even with the very high PSA. It may quite simply stay put.
2. The success rate of the radiation treatment isn't one hundred percent. I may undergo the treatment and, in a month, or in a year or two, learn that I have cancer of the bones (marrow, really), the brain, the liver—any organ one can name that one would like to have spared, every one having its origin in the prostate. Hence, I

am not throwing away an assured cure if I refuse the treatment.

3. I am in excellent health, except for the cancer. But I'm old. If the cancer is cured or driven underground for a sufficiently long time I am certain to get sick in some other way. It can be an unrelated cancer. It can be a stroke. I don't have heart disease, but that doesn't mean I can't have a stroke, the ultimate horror in my opinion, because it is so very likely to disable one. You've probably seen the infinite and heartbreaking variety of crippling punishments strokes inflict. That's one illness I don't want to endure.

4. The great "advantage" of cancers is that unless one goes down the path of more and more treatments, one keeps one's autonomy. One can decide when the curtain should come down. One is not at the mercy of children or friends.

I'll try to talk Dr. Klein into continuing his watchful waiting. And I'll hope for the best. Some more years of being no worse off physically or mentally than now.

As I pretty much expected, she replied by the briefest of affectionate messages, asking me to call at eleven in the evening, her time, the day after the election. We can't organize our lives by email, she said when I reached her. When can you come to Paris? I know it's a great deal to ask, I can imagine that you're tired.

Any day you like, I told her, for instance tomorrow!

No, no, come on Thursday or Friday, and don't forget that I love you.

Thursday, I replied, it's sooner!

Oh, and is your hotel nice? Will you have a nice room? Because I'd like to have lunch with you, late, so that you can get settled in properly before we meet. After lunch, I'll come to your hotel.

It was a cold but sunny day, atypical for Paris in November. I took a small suite with a terrace, not because I thought we'd have our coffee outside, but because the bedroom was large and both it and the living room were flooded with light. For the first time, she undressed entirely. As I caressed her I admired how youthful her body had remained. Not unchanged, but youthful, her skin clear, white, and soft, her stomach with just a little more fat on it, her marvelous little breasts, still like those of Gabrielle d'Estrée in the painting of her and her sister on a balcony that hangs in the Louvre. When she ordered me to take my clothes off, I saw the difference and was ashamed. How could she find the presence of my body pleasant, take my penis into her mouth or inside her. I was mostly sallow, covered with warts and suspect blemishes, dry and itchy. I was slender but flabby. I said nothing and redoubled my attention to her breasts, her clitoris. When she pulled my head down I complied with the relief that pilgrims must feel upon reaching the Holy

Land at the end of a long and perilous journey. She did not want me to take her, not just then, *pas tout de suite*, it was her turn, she wanted to do the adolescent stuff. We lay back later, leaning against the pillows that the hotel furnished in profusion.

Would it be totally decadent if I asked you to order champagne? she asked.

It would be delightful, I replied.

There were splits of champagne in the minibar, but I sensed that for her this was an occasion that transcended drinking whatever the minibar had to offer. I called room service and asked for a pink Laurent-Perrier I thought she'd like. She did. After I'd refilled her glass and she'd emptied it, she turned on her side, put her leg over mine, and said, I want to go on making love, but I must speak to you seriously first. I've thought a great deal about your email and your decision. I think your decision is right. It's the question of autonomy. I've thought about how it applies to my poor Hubert. Suppose he had not lost his mind, suppose he were not like a child, totally dependent on me, would he want to go on? And, in this regard, he is very lucky. I take very good care of him, I choose people who are extraordinarily nice to him, he lives in places—Anatole France and our house in the Poitou—that he has always known and loved. I think you fear that your situation might be worse. So, I can't help thinking that in a strange and cruel way you are right. Bravo, my darling Hugo! This has been a long speech. May I go on?

Yes, I whispered.

When you suggested that because you are lonely, and I am lonely, we could make each other happier if you came to live in Paris—much of the time—as my very special friend, I said don't, don't do it because you don't really belong here, you'd have no life of your own beyond our meetings in your garçonnière and our outings to the opera, ballet, what have you. Or perhaps I hesitated. It's no longer clear in my mind. I know one thing very clearly: I want you just the way we are. I want you as often as we don't tire of each other. Above all, without making any promises or big arrangements. So long as things are as they are. And when we can't be this way, we'll be friends. Best friends. *D'accord?* Now take me, take me as hard as you know how.

What was it about her? A magical potion that she secreted, Zerlina-like? I found I could, and no doubt because of what she had done for me before our champagne entr'acte, bring her to orgasm after orgasm and to exhaustion.

I had left the bottle in the ice bucket and poured us each a glass.

The deal is a perfect deal, I told her after a moment. I would like to know, if you think you can tell me, what has led you to propose it.

She remained silent for a while, and then asked, What if my answer seems brutal?

I'll take that risk, I replied.

All right, she said, it was thinking about Hubert and being responsible for him and how if I wasn't very careful I might become responsible for you as well. I don't think I could bear it. No one has enough strength. That's a danger independent of your cancer, since you have decided, and I completely believe you, not to let it turn you into an invalid. It's your age. As you wrote, if it's not one disease it will be another. If you hate what I've said, if you start to hate me, so be it. I've told you the truth.

It was my turn to be silent. Then I cradled her in my arms and told her that I thought I was falling in love with her all over again, because she was so intelligent, so honest, and because she was the best lay I'd ever had.

I remained in Paris a week, a week of lunches followed by hours of happiness in my hotel room. You're all fucked out, she observed, when the third day I remained limp as a dishcloth. But that doesn't matter. I've told you it doesn't. She was right. I think her pleasure was just as intense and perhaps so was mine. She invited me to spend a few days in Poitou over Christmas. I sensed the slight hesitation in her voice. I felt none whatever. I said we shouldn't do anything complicated. Audibly relieved, she told me that Hubert and she would return to Paris on the tenth of January. In that case, I exclaimed, I would come a couple of days later and stay long enough to be away from the U.S. on the day of Trump's inauguration. That's perfect, she replied, and then, caressing me, took back her agreement. That's not our deal, she whispered, do come if everything comes together, but no plans please, no elaborate plans. They're a trap. I don't want to take the bait.

Our new routine left my evenings free. I telephoned

Jacques Legrand and made a date to have dinner with him in Paris the next day.

I received a call myself that day, first thing in the morning, from the editor of the leading Zurich daily for whom I'd written short essays on Hillary and Trump. The most recent of these, on what he called the election night shock, I had emailed to him the day before. He liked the piece; he had liked the others; he wanted to tell me viva voce how much he liked my work and admired me and how he was taking advantage of our being for once in the same time zone. Then came the real purpose of the call: Would I write for his paper a short political piece on any subject that interested me every four to six weeks?

I had finished Bush/Cheney and had no other pending project. Why not do it, I thought, I may need this fellow's goodwill and help.

Accordingly, I said, I'd be delighted to do it, beginning let's say in mid-January. Would that be satisfactory?

Oh, yes, amply satisfactory.

There is a side benefit I'd like to ask for, I continued. May I count on your discretion?

Yes, absolutely yes.

All right. It may be that I will need the help of a Zurich doctor or clinic—I don't know how to describe it—if I found I was gravely ill with no prospect of recovery. Will you help me find the best person or the best clinic and to make the necessary arrangements?

My dear Herr Gardner, I hope it will never come to that but, if it does, you may count on me. One hundred percent.

I thanked him. This was what I hoped for. It was easier to do it, as he put it, viva voce than by email.

Jacques and I met at Au Petit Riche, a restaurant across the street from Salle Drouot distinguished by its Belle Époque décor and traditional cuisine. Jacques had become an habitué at a time when he was a regular at auctions of antique clocks and introduced me to it. I have since eaten there often, especially on Sundays when many other places I like in Paris are closed.

What good wind brings you to the Hexagon? he exclaimed, and how am I going to explain to Lucie why you haven't come to Bayeux? Quite seriously, I hope it isn't that you feel uneasy about driving after your last misadventure. You know, it's really quite possible to take the train. That's what I did today.

I assured him it was nothing of the sort, that I had to drive everywhere in the Hamptons. That's America, you know. It's that or my old three-speed bicycle, and of the two I think taking my car is less dangerous. There is a nice reason for my being here. I'm seeing Jeanne.

Seeing Jeanne! Jacques exploded. She must be still *une très bonne affaire*. Congratulations, old man! Why do I say "old man"? I should say, congratulations, Casanova! Of course, that charming young person must have been dying of boredom. She was for years, you know, with—he named a member of the French Academy—I think it started well before anyone, including Hubert and Jeanne, realized Hubert was losing his mind, and it was generally considered that they were a very elegant pair. The great historian and *la petite comtesse*! And soon the Almanach de Gotha husband was lost in a world of his own! Then *monsieur l'Académicien français* took the bit between his teeth. He bucked and threw Jeanne over for a twenty-years-younger Dutch beauty.

I didn't want to hear more.

Yes, I said, I know the outline of this dreary story. Poor Jeanne had no luck there.

Neither did the great historian. Jacques laughed. The young beauty ditched him in turn for a seriously rich Russian!

Let's order dinner, I suggested. We each had one whiskey and I was beginning to feel that it was not prudent to continue. The choice of what we were going to eat and the wine to accompany the meal took us no time; we both knew the menu and the wine list. Please bring the wine right away, Jacques instructed the waiter.

America, America, Jacques intoned, God shed his grace on thee . . . It will be a changed America with Mr. Trump. Ha! Getting a rest from Mr. Obama and the twenty-second century. You know the iron rule: For every action there is an equal and opposite reaction. Your country needs to return to its roots. I don't need to spell out for you what they are. It needs to remember that it's great and that it doesn't have to spend its time apologizing. You are the country who saved us in the Second World War. Take the GIs who are buried in the cemetery we have visited, and before that stormed our beaches: I don't need to tell you that there weren't many Hispanics or blacks—excuse me, African Americans— among them. You did the same in the First World War. Again, not too many Hispanics or blacks singing, "Over there, over there, send the word, send the word over there to beware...."

I began to feel immeasurably tired and did what all idiots do at such moments. I motioned for the waiter to refill my glass, emptied it, and asked him to bring another bottle. And I looked at my dear old friend Jacques. As I had already determined in Bayeux, he had changed but not very much. Grown older, yes, I said to myself wearily, but it's the same sharply drawn profile, the same fine mouth, the same smile. Down to what he wore, gray suit, blue shirt, navy-blue knit tie, black shoes, the uniform of a bourgeois of his generation, a civil servant, it was all there, it all fit. I smiled at him.

He smiled back, and said, I don't think I've convinced you.

You haven't, I said. Trump is a racist. The country's demographic makeup has changed. A racist in the White House will exacerbate our racial problems, lead to great troubles.

You'll find out you're wrong, Jacques replied. I'm the least racist of men, the family has been in the colonies, we had large properties in Algeria, we know how to get along with blacks and Muslims. The key is that they must respect the rules of our society and adapt to our culture. If they can't or won't, out they go!

I see, I said. But the system doesn't seem to be working any too well these days. *Les cités*, the slums, the crime rate, the terrorist attacks. I could go on.

We're governed by wimps. That will change.

In the next year's election?

Yes. There will be no more Hollande or anyone like him at the Élysée but someone who knows how to govern.

Who is that?

Fillon, of course. A Catholic, a real Frenchman, a man with a vision of France for the French. You'll see.

Jacques would have surely found a proverb for the occasion. Perhaps, *Il ne faut pas vendre la peau de l'ours avant de l'avoir tué*. Don't count your chickens before they're hatched. I could not repress a feeling of satisfaction months later when one corrupt scheme Fillon had concocted for his own enrichment after another was revealed and put an inglorious end to his candidacy.

That lay in the future.

That evening, at Au Petit Riche, I remembered Jeanne's telling me he had moved way over to the right, and how I wasn't surprised to hear it. His uncles were Algérie *française*, revanchists who could not forgive de Gaulle for his "betrayal" of French *colons* who considered Algeria their land and despised the peace he made with Algerian revolutionaries. I suppose I assumed that he was successively for Pompidou and Giscard d'Estaing. These were matters

I was almost sure we had never really talked about. Politics and political analysis were my profession, and I didn't much care to discuss them with someone who wasn't a pro.

I had three more afternoons with Jeanne left to me. I wondered whether I was in love, and whether she was putting the same question to herself. We stuck to our pact, though, above all no seriousness and no plans. But as I left Paris I did so with the hope that the plan she had refused to approve, my projected return to Paris in January, would after all come to pass.

XII

M Y WATCHFUL UROLOGIST—I have not figured
out whether I should refer to Dr. Klein as my
urologist or my oncologist—seemed to keep an
eye also on my comings and goings. The day after my return
to New York I received an email from the hospital directing
me to log on to its website to read a message from him. Did
I know my username and password? No, I didn't, but I had
asked the hospital's site to remember them. Relieved not to
be obliged to go through the contortions of recovering first
one and then the other, I got to the message center or whatever it was called and learned that I was to call the doctor's
secretary to make an appointment. I followed instructions
and was told by that lady to report to the doctor's office at
the hospital the following day, eight-thirty in the morning.
The curmudgeon coiled up inside me wished to inquire why
it had been necessary for the hospital to dispatch an email
that sent me scrambling to read a message on its website
when it would have sufficed for her to give me a call, thus

saving me time and sparing me twenty minutes of need-
less irritation. I told the old fellow to shut up. The secretary
was a nice lady; it was not she but some high-salary geeks
in the hospital's Internet technology department who had
invented that idiotic system, and my self-interest required
me to remain on good terms with her.

It was what I had half expected would eventually happen:
the doctor was about to perform what he so politely called a
procedure! Taking note of my surprise, he asked whether I
had not been told that was what we were doing this morning. No, but that was all right; the army had taught me
many useful maxims, *Don't fight the problem* being one of
them. Would I like to be sedated? Not particularly, let's go!

After I had rested and been fed a fig newton and cran-
berry juice, the doctor reviewed his findings.

There is no indication of metastasis, he told me, but that's
subject to my study of the images we've taken. What I'm
saying now is based only on what I observed on the screen
during the procedure.

Ah, yes, I had watched him out of the corner of my eye
making faces and humming to himself as he peered at the
screen and directed the torpedolike object moving hither
and thither inside me.

That doesn't mean, Hugo, he continued, that you should
say yippee! and do nothing. If you do nothing, the odds will
be against you. If you enter treatment now, your cancer can
be cured. How about it, Hugo?

I'd come to like the guy and didn't want to hurt his feelings or make him think I wasn't taking his advice seriously. The former risk, I realized, was remote. As for the latter, it couldn't be helped. My mind was made up.

You have explained it all very clearly, I said, and I'm very grateful, but I really don't want to do the radiation. Your cure may turn out to be a prelude to other illnesses and new dilemmas. Let's roll the dice. We both know how it will end whatever we do—in exactly the same place.

Excuse me, Hugo, but this is nihilistic crap. Why don't you say straight out that you're tired of life and want to commit suicide?

I could have shaken my head, thanked him, and gone home, but I felt the need to explain myself. I really didn't want him to think I was nuts or lacking in respect.

Because that's simply not true, I replied. Please don't feel concerned. I'm not tired of life. I love life even though I'm lonely and often unhappy. But I want to live on my own terms. That means being capable of thought, of making my own decisions, of moving around without a walker or wheelchair. I'm accustomed to chronic pain in my lower back and the aches and pains in this and the other joint that come and go, but I wouldn't want to live with great pain. Doesn't that make sense to you?

He didn't bother to answer.

At the kosher restaurant a few blocks up the avenue from the hospital I had a revoltingly large hot-pastrami-on-rye sandwich and a beer. It was a treat to which I looked forward after each visit to Dr. Klein or the very nice doctor who pumped steroids into the neighborhood of my spine. Two-thirty in the afternoon. I called Gloria, my Bridgehampton housekeeper, told her I was driving out to the country, and asked her to open the house and turn up the heat to sixty-eight, and to pick up and put in the fridge some orange juice, bread, butter, and eggs.

When I awoke the next morning, I thought I might still be in a long-forgotten happy dream. Gloria had been busy, waxing furniture, dusting books, vacuuming every nook and cranny. The house smelled very good. It was a cold, sunny day. After breakfast, I took a stroll in the garden. Like the house, it was in perfect order, neatly raked and clean, meticulously gotten ready for the winter. The telephone and the Internet worked. Instead of going to get the paper in Bridgehampton, I read the press on my laptop. Right there was the bad dream, the nightmare from which there was no waking. I had supposed I'd have lunch at the Candy Kitchen, but I changed my mind. It was too pleasant inside. I ate scrambled eggs, washed them down with a half bottle of Chianti, and was grateful to Gloria for having bought grapes and McIntosh apples without having been asked. The dishes could wait. My nap couldn't. I went upstairs to my bedroom, brushed my teeth, undressed, and got under the covers. I was lucky, I thought, to own such a beautiful house filled with objects I loved, to have come back to it after many weeks and be spared unpleasant surprises, to find it just the way it should be. It would be hard to say goodbye.

The phone rang just before nine, waking me. I might have slept through the night otherwise, or as much of it as my nocturnal leg cramps and micturition permitted. It was Roddy.

I'm glad I've found you, Dad, he said, you left a couple of messages saying you'd call again, but you didn't. Anyway, you're back. Have you had a good time? Are you all right? Why didn't you call again the way you said?

What a lot of questions! I didn't call again at first because I understood you were very busy and then decided to wait for you to call me when you had time. Yes, I'm back. Yes, I had a good time. I'm fine but dead tired. That's the great discovery.

You should get some sleep. Jet lag!

I was asleep. And I may well go back to sleep after we hang up. But I want to hear your news.

He told me that the new job was all right—so far—his colleagues pleasant, his office comfortable. He was glad he'd made the move. Carla and the kids were fine. They'd had Thanksgiving with Mom, the whole gang. Great fun.

That's nice to hear, I said, and asked about Barbara.

Same as ever, he said. All worked up about the new porch membership policy at the country club. Really worked up. Dr. De Graff came with her. All is quiet on that front, or so it seemed to me. Honest, Dad, your daughter and my sister isn't getting any smarter. It may be something in the Wellesley town water. Mom's self-appointed champion! A country club busybody! When will you be back in the city? I'd like to see you. Or maybe you could drive over and have dinner with Carla and the kids. That would be great, especially if you can do it on the weekend.

That's the nicest idea I've heard in a good while, I said. I'll let you know about the weekend.

Nine-fifteen. I felt newly cheerful and hungry. It was probably too late to go to dinner in Sag Harbor. I drove to Bridgehampton, found a parking place, and got a table at the steak house a couple of doors down from Candy Kitchen. The noise would have made any attempt at conversation unthinkable, but I wasn't going to talk to anybody. All I wanted was a large rare hamburger and some red wine. These were satisfactory, but they took their time arriving. While I waited, sipping a bourbon on the rocks, I reviewed my last exchange with the urologist. I told him I loved life. Was that true? As always since Valerie left, when I thought about my existence in general terms, two great sorrows came into focus. First, lying in bed alone night after night and remembering the many years of fondling Valerie before we fell asleep and when we woke up, of believing that she loved or liked me as much as I loved her. It wasn't so much a matter of missing sex, although I would have very much wanted to have that continue. It was her absence. Second, my failures as a father and grandfather. Rod and I got along about as well as my father had gotten along with me: pleasant but not particularly affectionate contacts, and a sense that in a pinch I could depend on him. His being able to count on me was beyond doubt. Barbara? I was bewildered by her behavior, unable to recall when, or through what action or inaction, I had so offended her. Was there some way I could make amends? I doubted it. If a remedy existed, Rod would know what it was and would have surely told me what to do. Perhaps she was possessed. I could imagine one or more of our Puritan ancestors inhabiting the North Shore of Massachusetts Bay Colony in the 1680s and '90s pointing a bony, crooked finger at her and whispering, Oh that poor creature she is driven by the Evil One. As for my grandchildren, I thought I understood what had happened. Barbara's hysterical—no other word fit—resentment of me made relations with her children pretty much impossible. On top of that, Valerie was a hyperactive grandmother. She had left no place or role for me while we were together. Now that I was alone, I didn't know how to create one. Perhaps that could change.

Thereupon the wine arrived. I had ordered a Napa Valley Syrah. The waiter uncorked the bottle. I tasted and said, Please go ahead. No, I wasn't getting drunk or even high, but a feeling of unquestioned happiness overwhelmed me. I had not lied to the doctor. There were pages and pages in my ledger where nothing but joys and sweetness had been entered. What were they? A modest sort of love of nature untethered to any great knowledge or ambitions. Joys derived quite simply from my garden, from the will to live and the herculean strength of certain flowering bushes, rhododendrons being foremost among them; from gold-finches' and cardinals' enthusiastic visits to the bird feeder; from walks on the Atlantic beaches in Bridgehampton and Sagaponack, and memories of plunging into the surf; from writing when it goes well; from certain books and operas; and, very reliably, from good food and drink. *The best things in life are free . . .* No, in my case they required a good deal of money, but I thought I would not run out before the abhorred shears slit my thin-spun life. To be sure, if those cavorting cancer cells (the alliteration made me giggle) have any kindness in them and know what's good for Roddy and Barbara, they'll get a move on soon!

I decided to have coffee at home, called for the check, paid, and got into my car. You're a strange fellow, a Voice remarked. You're happy, let's be more accurate, mostly happy, but you've refused to submit to a treatment that has a good chance of curing you. The doctor hasn't asked this question, but I will: How do you feel about leaving this life, about entering into what looks like a suicide pact with yourself? It's a good question, I replied, and here is the answer: I feel immense regret. Vast regret. As vast as the ocean. I really like it here. I want to stay. I don't want to leave. But, but, but, as I told the doctor, I only want to stay if it's on my terms. The Voice was unconvinced. Have you thought of what you might do if the cancer cells stay put, but you have a stroke? Yes, if the stroke doesn't incapacitate me and the neurologist doesn't convince me that the chances of another stroke are minimal, I will leave in some relatively painless way. Let me state a general rule: I don't want to stick around and be a pain in the ass for myself or others.

There was a telephone message waiting for me at home. From Roddy: Dad, I forgot to tell you. You've got to watch *Saturday Night Live* this evening. It comes on at eleven. It will be mostly about your favorite president-in-waiting. I think you'll laugh your head off.

My son is a very nice guy, I said out loud. Let's not forget that.

I didn't laugh much watching Alec Baldwin be Trump. I was horrified. The president-elect too busy retweeting, yes, retweeting, random messages to listen to an intelligence briefing! Yes, the segment was brilliant. Yes, it was wildly funny. But it was also, in my opinion, without doubt the image of what was to come. Some seventy-seven thousand voters in Wisconsin, Michigan, and Pennsylvania had delivered the country into the hands of a conceited, malevolent asshole.

The telephone rang at nine the next morning as I was working my way through the paid obituaries in the Sunday *NYT*. Relief mixed with disappointment: thus far, I hadn't come across anyone I knew. I picked up the receiver and pressed the TALK button without looking at the caller-identification window. It was Penny, breathless even at this early hour. She had been calling my NYC number and, unable to reach me there, tried Bridgehampton on the off chance I'd be here. Would I come to dinner that very evening? Just you and me and an old friend of yours. No, I won't tell you who. I'll keep you guessing. Or perhaps we'll be four, if I can get Sally Parker. Eight o'clock? *Merde,* I muttered to myself, I really don't want to do this. Nothing is worse than mystery old friends. But the idea of seeing Sally swayed me. I told Penny I'd be there with bells on. I believe I actually said that.

The little note of triumph I thought I heard in Penny's voice when she mentioned the old friend found its explanation as soon as I stepped into her living room. With his back to the fire was Archbold Newsome, one class behind me at college, an acquaintance, yes, but hardly a friend. I recalled reading a couple of years back a notice concerning his wife, a Radcliffe girl whom I also knew, who was said to have succumbed after a long and valiant battle with cancer. There was no mention of surviving children. A conspicuously rich heiress, she'd been the object of stagy and assiduous attentions of a coterie of voluble and, so it seemed to me, overexcited ephebes, foremost among whom was Archie. I don't believe that the word "homophobia" was known to me, but that nameless sentiment, along with anti-Semitism, was rampant among my contemporaries, and according to the gossip of those who claimed to understand such matters, neither Archie nor his friends were interested in girls. Therefore, it was postulated, they were fortune hunters, a supposition, when you think of it, perfectly consistent with

Archie's being rich himself and having rich parents. Rich people like other rich people. This old stuff came up unsolicited from wherever sour trivia are stored and gave me the basis for an instant reappraisal of this "old friend." Archie looked good, far better than sixty years ago: he had taken on just enough weight to look solid, the arms that embraced me bore witness to a regime of working out with dumbbells, he had a healthy tan, a fine haircut, and a tweed jacket I liked.

It's been much too long! he announced.

I agreed, told him I knew about Lilly, had been truly sad to read about her, and hoped he had forgiven me for not writing. He gave me another hug by way of answer and rapidly explained that he'd run into Penny at dinner at the Hortons in the city—I'd no idea who they were—that he invited her to lunch the next day, that once again it clicked between them, *et voilà*! He was retired, just like everybody else, and lonely. Just like Penny! You know that Lilly and I had no children. With Penny, it has been just like the old times.

Congratulations, I said with entire sincerity, congratulations to both of you!

Whatever had been snickered at as his effeminate aspect was gone, perhaps the effect of age, perhaps it had never existed. In any case, it meant nothing. What I knew about gays at the time could be reduced to a couple of dirty jokes I no longer remembered. I certainly didn't know that even the most masculine men could be sexually drawn to other men. My curiosity was piqued, however, by his saying that "it" had clicked "again." What the devil was he talking about?

Penny enlightened me over coffee, having drawn me to sit beside her on a chaise longue. Archie, she said, was going to live with her in Springs, and she'd live with him in his apartment in the city. He has, of course, his house in Millbrook, but he hates it there. The whole point was that Lilly kept horses and hunted as long as she could. Without her, it makes no sense. He thinks he'll sell it.

It was her turn to receive my congratulations. Again, I was totally sincere. Loneliness is awful, I said. You're lucky. And you and Archie wasted no time. Hasn't this been remarkably sudden? A real *coup de foudre*!

She laughed and, I believe, blushed. Not really, she whispered. Archie and I had a thing going long ago, when Lilly first fell sick, and you know... my own relations with Dwight—the less said about them the better. It's really a homecoming.

Penny had double-crossed me, saying there would be only three or four of us at dinner. She had invited another couple, the former ambassador to Turkey and his wife. It turned out that the ambassador and Archie were intimate friends, and the hazard of seating and the flow of the conversation at table prevented me from exchanging more than a few words with Sally. When we got up, she told me she had come to Penny's via Uber; she disliked making the drive at night, particularly if she had a drink or two too many. Would I take her home? Naturally, I was delighted.

I guess Penny has done very well for herself, she observed, once we were in the car. He's presentable. Looks healthy.

Has an apartment and a house of his own, so he hasn't moved in with her just to have a roof over his head. Some people have all the luck. I hate being alone, and I've been alone ever since the dreaded Ted and I split. What do you think is the matter with me?

Absolutely nothing, I replied. Perhaps you're too choosy.

Perhaps, she said. At least I have my four-legged Hugo and you, big cousin Hugo. Why don't you come over to play with little Hugo? He's more mature now and very well behaved. Would you like to have lunch tomorrow? If you come a little early, say at twelve, we'll go for a walk on the beach before we sit down at table.

I had done everything that needed to be done for my book, and I'd gotten myself organized to write the first essay for the Zurich paper. There was no reason not to jump at this invitation.

Thank you! I'll be there.

The ocean was just over the dune from Sally's house. The little Frenchie didn't need a leash. At the word "beach" pronounced by Sally, he was off like a shot and we had to quicken our pace not to lose sight of him.

He does all his little business at the beach, she told me. Never in the garden. He doesn't think that's civilized. If it's blowing a gale or raining hard, I have to take him out on the road. If that isn't true elegance, you find a better example!

The little business being done, Sally picked it up with a

plastic bag. I had no acquaintance with this aspect of eti-
quette, but somehow understood I was to take the bag from
Sally and carry it. Both she and the little Frenchie made me
feel I'd done the right thing.

Now you call him, Hugo, Sally said, let's see whether he
comes. Of course, he didn't, whereupon she gave me her dog
whistle and told me to try it and, when he comes, give him a
treat. It worked once and then again. Bravo, said Sally, now
if you want you can take him out for walks. Really, there is
no risk on this beach. No road he can wander off to, no dan-
gers at all, and he's too prudent to go into the waves. By the
way, are you going to be here at Christmas?

Very likely, unless there is a snowstorm.

Then come to Christmas Eve dinner or Christmas Day
lunch or both. Don't make that face! We won't be singing
carols, and unless my sons honor me by a visit—believe me
I don't count on it—we might well be alone.

Sally, I said, Sally, we've known each other such a long
time. You know I'm not the holiday-celebration type. Mercy!

No mercy at all. I'll count on you. All right? You don't
need to say a word. Just nod your head once.

I did as I was told.

And are you going back to Paris or Vienna or wherever?

Paris is a possibility, for a few days in January. I'm not
sure.

Well, for reasons I'll disclose another day, I want you to be
here. Understood?

As I was thanking her after coffee, and getting ready to

leave, she said, Why don't you invite me to dinner? We have such a good time together.

I replied I'd love to, and asked: When?

Friday?

That's a terrible evening to go out, I said, the noise in restaurants is so loud I won't hear a word you say. Would Sunday be all right?

No, she said, shaking her head, I'd like it to be sooner. Friday. Can't you invite me to dinner at your house?

Perfect! If you don't mind store-bought fried chicken or the equivalent.

I laughed on my way home. An invitation to walk that adorable little bulldog, a chance to have dinner with that beautiful cousin of mine I'd always liked, for a wretched old guy, a tattered coat upon a stick, I was for the moment doing well.

The next day, I opened my laptop after breakfast to check my emails and saw a message from Jeanne. I have to speak to you, it read, I'm at home.

It was sent less than half an hour earlier. I called her number. She answered the phone herself.

There were no preliminaries.

Hugo, she said, I thought I should tell you right away, and I thought it was better to speak than to write. I've gotten back together with Yves—that was the name of the illustrious French academician. You know that he left me for another woman. I'm not sure that I've told you that a few years later she left him, brutally. Since then, Yves's wife died. He is all alone and not well. He has a weak heart and weak lungs. Perhaps the beginnings of emphysema. He needs me. And I love him. I've never stopped loving him. Getting back together with him made me see that the times you and I had together last month were a wonderful diversion. That's all. I'm grateful for them. I hope you will understand—you always do—and that we will remain friends.

I'm not sure what I felt. That I was about to have an unbearable headache? That I had been unable to understand what she said? That some unspecified misfortune had befallen me? I was so confused that I remained silent.

Hugo, she insisted, you did hear what I said, didn't you? I'm back with Yves. You do understand?

I pulled myself together, and said, Yes, of course. I wish you luck. Are you leaving Hubert?

I can't. But depending on Yves's health I may have to arrange to have him move in with us. It would make such good sense. This apartment is so large. And, of course, in Poitou, there is the whole château. He could have a wing all to himself! We'll have to see.

Had she gone insane? I couldn't resist making a crack.

A field hospital, I commented slowly in tones of persiflage, with you as the head nurse! As I said, good luck!

You're a *vrai salaud,* a real son of a bitch, she shouted into the phone, and hung up.

The last time she called me that she also slapped my face. Could it be that she was right?

Sink into the earth? Leave for the city, disconnect the Internet at the apartment, block the telephone, have food brought in? How was I to hide my shame? That is how I perceived the horror of what had happened to me. Gloria was due any minute. Not wanting to face her or anyone else, I left the breakfast dishes on the table, skipped the ritual of brushing my teeth, and drove to the beach. A huge walk over the hard sand, from the Bridgehampton beach club all the way to Georgica. Not a soul anywhere. I half wished I had Hugo the Frenchie or another nice dog with me, but maybe it was better this way. No responsibility. No one to pick up after, no one to call to heel if he wandered off, no one making goo-goo eyes at me and asking for a treat. At some point, where the ocean had sculpted a shelf in the beach, I lay down and stared at the sky. Where was the shame? I asked myself after a while. Her dropping me like a used Kleenex, in her father's memorable phrase? What of it? She'd picked me up, shamelessly and unexpectedly, less than two months ago. I'd gone to see her on my sentimental journey, invited her to dinner, and found myself in her demented husband's library doing oral sex with Madame la comtesse. So far as she was concerned, no big deal! Made up for a humiliating memory of my own behavior. Yves the academician—how could I come near imagining the bonds that had linked them, the meaning he had given to her starved life with the descendant of crusaders? She swallowed her pride to take

Yves back now—I was a pig not to be glad for her and offer good wishes like a real friend.

A few more thoughts like this, I said to myself, and you'll go bonkers or volunteer to work in a leper colony if leper colonies still exist.

I got up, turned toward the dune, urinated easily and abundantly—how much longer will those frigging cells allow me to enjoy such simple pleasures—and, calling cadence, quick marched home. Heidi, Heidi, Heidi hi, Heidi, Heidi, Heidi ho, cancer cells are on the go! Count cadence, count cadence, count cadence, count!

Long experience of dealing with myself has taught me that I should act quickly on good resolutions. Not particularly because I'm likely to change my mind. More probably, I may quite simply run out of steam. Never get around to doing whatever it was I was planning to do.

It was still early enough in Paris for me to call my place du Palais-Bourbon florist. A very special plant, I told her, for Madame de Viry, very special but not an orchid.

I didn't want to remind her of the occasion on which I had last sent her one.

I have a superb white azalea tree, she informed me. I'm certain that Madame la comtesse will appreciate it.

So be it, I said, and I dictated the card to go with the plant: Best wishes for good luck and happiness, straight from the heart.

———

Will my story have a happy ending? Look around you: all lives end more or less badly. Why should mine be an exception?

I got the fried chicken at the very last minute, so it would be crisp and still warm, smoked salmon that I decided to serve as a first course, cold spicy noodles to go with the chicken, muscat grapes, and a big slice of Stilton. Sherry-Lehmann had recently delivered a case of Chinon I liked. I opened a bottle and put another one on the sideboard, just in case. It was a cold night. I lit the fire in the library and made sure that the firewood had been laid correctly in the dining room. I'd light it when we sat down. I could not think when I had a guest to dinner at this house last. Of course, when Valerie was still here. That surely accounted for some of my nervousness. I didn't know what else to call it. And there was no denying it: I was childishly glad that the guest was my little cousin Sally.

She ate and drank like a trouper and claimed everything on the table was exactly what she had hoped for.

Now, now Sally, I said, there was a time when I would have cooked a good dinner. Perhaps grilled a steak. I'm out of practice!

As we talked, we both realized how little I knew about her life as a married woman. She was, after all, give or take a year, twenty-five years younger! I'd come back from Paris to go to her wedding in Boston. It was natural that I should. My parents were still alive. I had had countless dinners at her parents' house when I was in college and had spent an occasional Saturday or Sunday with them when my prep school let us out for the weekend. She was my favorite young relative. Then she disappeared with her husband to the West Coast.

You don't know what happened? she asked.

I shook my head.

I thought everyone knew, she cried, after twenty years of marriage he decided the time had come for him to be himself. In his case, it meant to tell me he has been suffering from gondor dysphoria that's the term he used, I had to look it up afterward!—that it has become clear that he is really a woman, and he's going to transition! He's announcing this urbi et orbi, just so there is no misunderstanding, and he has already told the boys! I said that's what you've discovered after twenty years of marriage, two children, a normal life? I think I ranted more than that, and concluded by asking a really stupid question: Why can't you just go on the way you are, and cross-dress or whatever?

So what did he say?

He drew himself up to his full six feet three inches and declared: I can't go on living a lie! That's when I broke a huge Venini vase over his head. He needed ten stitches. Of course, that's nothing in comparison with what he has gone through since. Not just hormone therapy and breast enlargement, but castration, penis removal, and, according to what my older son says, the construction of a vulva. Can you imagine it? I mean, if he wants to be screwed, there is another way!

That story is just too postmodern for me. Something tells me that if that is how he felt, you are better off now that he has gone away and done it. One can only hope he thinks he is better off too.

I've run myself ragged trying to think about it, she replied. All I'm left knowing is that I'm very lonely. I have no one. Son number one lives in Singapore. Son number two lives in Hawaii. They're both married, without children. Don't tell anyone, but it's a fact: they didn't ask Ted or me to their weddings. I go back to the same thing: I'm lonely. I promise that I don't have any sort of unpleasant body odor, my breath smells clean, as you see I'm a member of the clean plate club, and I have good table manners! Perhaps I'm not rich enough. There are guys who know my family, who know about Ted, and think I'm loaded. Then they run a check and find out that not all that shines is gold. So, even if they've laid me, off they go.

I made coffee on my new espresso machine and we moved to the library.

What a good fire, she said, what a nice room, what a good host! Do you think this lonely girl could have a brandy or a single malt scotch?

I poured us both a scotch. Then we had another. Then Sally said, I should go home, but I'm too drunk. You must have a guest room somewhere in this lovely house. Could your cousin Sally spend the night? And perhaps have breakfast?

I said the answer to both questions was yes, and that

I could provide a toothbrush, toothpaste, and one of my L.L. Bean shirts that might do in the place of pajamas.

That's all right. She giggled. I foresaw that I might have to ask to sleep over. If you are kind enough to go to my car, Cousin Hugo, you'll find in the back seat a satchel with all I need.

She came downstairs next morning just as I came home with scones I picked up for our breakfast and the *NYT*.

What a good sleep, she said, what a beautiful kitchen, what a lovely smell of coffee, and what yummy-looking scones! What more could a wayward girl ask?

She wore a white peignoir over white pajamas; she looked fresh as dew, perhaps because she had clearly just taken a shower.

We ate our breakfast silently, sharing the newspaper. After her second or third cup of coffee she said, Cousin Hugo, I have a proposal I'd like to submit. Here it is: As I explained at too great length yesterday at dinner, I'm very lonely. One very annoying aspect of my condition is that I have no one to take me to things—you know, parties and dinners where you are expected to bring someone, or the theater, or the opera. Would you become my official beau? It would be so suitable. Please say yes!

But I don't like large cocktail parties and dinners, darling cousin Sally! You know that.

Oh, but I'd keep that to a bare minimum. And you could

always say no if you found whatever it was too boring. But I'd like to stay with you in the city. I don't think I've been to your apartment. I'm sure though you have a guest room as nice as the one here. And I'd like you to take me out in the city. I won't be a burden, Hugo, I'll pay my own way.

Now you're being silly, I said. If I take my little cousin Sally to dinner or the opera she'll be my guest.

I thought you'd say that. You're so old-fashioned. And then from time to time if we feel like it, if the mood is right, we could pet. That's also old-fashioned, dear Hugo, and it could be so nice!

She got up from her chair and before I could understand what she was doing sat down in my lap and put her arms around my neck.

Doesn't this feel nice?

It did. She was light, warm, and sweet smelling. I told her so. And then I told her we could have a deal, but it couldn't include sex, however much I'd like it. I was too old. It couldn't work; it couldn't end well.

But it could include this? she asked, nestling more comfortably. Making each other feel good? Because if it can, if you say yes, I'll throw in something you cannot reject, I'll share with you the custody of my little French bulldog. Now do I have a deal?

Yes, I said, you do. You most certainly do.

A NOTE ABOUT THE AUTHOR

Louis Begley's previous novels are *Killer's Choice; Kill and Be Killed; Killer, Come Hither; Memories of a Marriage; Schmidt Steps Back; Matters of Honor; Shipwreck; Schmidt Delivered; Mistler's Exit; About Schmidt; As Max Saw It; The Man Who Was Late;* and *Wartime Lies,* which won the PEN/Hemingway Award and the Irish Times/Aer Lingus International Fiction Prize. His work has been translated into fourteen languages. He is a member of the American Academy of Arts and Letters.

A NOTE ON THE TYPE

The text in this book was set in Miller, a transitional-style typeface designed by Matthew Carter (b. 1937) with assistance from Tobias Frere-Jones and Cyrus Highsmith of the Font Bureau. Modeled on the roman family of fonts popularized by Scottish type foundries in the nineteenth century, Miller is named for William Miller, founder of the Miller & Richard foundry of Edinburgh.